THE REDEMPTION TRAIL

Ex-outlaw Sam Hethridge has quit the bank-heisting game and rides into Indian Territory to seek work as a ranch hand. But his chance for a quiet life ends when he gets involved in a range war. With the help of Chester Willis, a young greenhorn US marshal, Sam takes on the land-grabbing rancher Silas Ketchum and his hired guns in a fight to the death for the right of the sodbusters to stay on their land. For once in his life, Sam finds himself fighting on the side of the law. Now, perhaps, there will be redemption for him!

ELLIOT CONWAY

THE REDEMPTION TRAIL

Complete and Unabridged

LINFORD
Leicester

First published in Great Britain in 2004 by
Robert Hale Limited
London

First Linford Edition
published 2005
by arrangement with
Robert Hale Limited
London

British Library CIP Data

Conway, Elliot
  The redemption trail.—Large print ed.—
Linford western library
1. Western stories
2. Large type books
I. Title
823.9'14 [F]

ISBN 1–84395–802–3

Published by
F. A. Thorpe (Publishing)
Anstey, Leicestershire

Set by Words & Graphics Ltd.
Anstey, Leicestershire
Printed and bound in Great Britain by
T. J. International Ltd., Padstow, Cornwall

This book is printed on acid-free paper

For the old Gringo on the occasion
of his 80th birthday

1

Kate Fischer watched the rider weaving his way through the small stand of cottonwoods on her side of the creek. It wasn't usual for her to have visitors, her place being well back from the main trail that ran close to the Canadian in this section of the Nations. The rider could be a marshal working out of Fort Smith, Arkansas, one of Judge Parker's manhunters who upheld the law, what little there was of it, in the Nations. More likely, Kate opined, the man could be seeking directions to Belle Starr's holding further west along the Canadian.

Kate reached down for the shotgun leaning against the front wall of the shack thumbing back both hammers. Mrs Belle Starr, or Mrs Blue Duck, as she sometimes favoured being called, was noted in the territory for running an open house for bank robbers, cattle thieves and suchlike lawless men whom Judge Parker would like to see swinging on his gallows back there in Fort Smith. And she was a widow woman living on her own, though longways past her bloom of youth, if she ever had any girlish flush, Kate thought wryly, as working as a short-time girl in sporting houses in Kansas trail-end towns servicing the needs of the wild Texas drovers when they hit town soon knocked the shine off a young girl's features. In spite of that she could still be lusted after by men who had been too busy dodging marshals' posses to have had time for a few hours of paid female companionship.

Sam Hethridge, two weeks out of the Kansas State Pen after serving ten years for bank and stage robberies while a member of the Cal Butler gang, saw the shotgun swing in his direction. He cursed softly. He'd had his fill of gunplay. The last raid the gang had attempted had turned into one deadly

2

and bloody balls-up. He had been the lucky one, the only one still alive to do his ten-year stretch in the Pen; the rest of the boys had got themselves shallow graves in a Kansas trail town Boot Hill.

Cal had planned to raid the Drovers Bank at Newton, Kansas, but somehow the law had got to know of the gang's intentions. Marshal's deputies were lying in wait for them, on flat roofs, side alleys, covering the gang with their rifles as they rode into town.

'Sam, you and Peck look after the horses,' Cal Butler had said, confident taking the bank's cash would be a walk over. 'Millar, stay outside the door and put off any customers comin' in,' Cal grinned. 'The rest of us will go inside and have words with the manager about arrangin' a substantial withdrawal.'

Cal hadn't known it right then but that was the last order he would dish out. And he wouldn't smile again this side of Hell's gates.

As Cal and the 'cash-withdrawal boys' were about to step on to the bank's porch all hell broke loose, rifles cutting loose at them from all directions. A hail of lead cut down Cal and the boys on the porch like ripened corn sliced by a reaper, killing them several times over. He and Peck, sheltered partly by the rearing and high-kicking frightened horses, managed to pull out their pistols and fire back at the lawmen.

Somehow Peck had got astride his horse, then Sam heard him cry out in pain and in the few seconds left before he was shot down he saw Peck's body with a leg trapped in a stirrup iron being dragged along Main Street by his spooked horse. Then he did some crying and groaning of his own on being hit by at least four shells. After that everything went blank and it was several days before he remembered anything about the small massacre, his recollecting being done in a doctor's surgery, guarded by two armed deputies. Yes, sir, Sam thought, he didn't favour having more lead in his hide.

That it was a woman holding a gun on him didn't calm nerves any. A double-barrelled shotgun in the hands of a 6-year-old kid at close range, was a killing or painfully maiming weapon. He tugged on his right rein as he approached the shack so that the big fiery red ball of the dying sun was at his back. His ploy worked: he could see the woman raise a hand to shield her eyes from the glare. Being an indistinct target, Sam hoped it would give him time to get close enough to tell the woman he was no threat to her.

Kate muttered several unlady-like curse words. She couldn't fire the shotgun with one hand. She stepped further back under the porch roof to escape the blinding light.

Kate could see her unwelcome visitor's face clearly now. A gaunt, hard-eyed-visaged man, yet surprisingly pale for an outdoor man. But not for one who had spent sometime in a prison cell, she thought worriedly.

'I mean you no harm, ma'am,' Sam

called out, as he drew up his horse. 'My mount's picked up a stone in his right foreleg hoof. I don't want him to go lame on me so when I saw your chimney smoke from the trail I cut across this way thinkin' there'd be a tool of sorts here I could use to prise out the stone.' Sam smiled reassuringly. 'I'm on my way to the Double Star ranch; I've heard that the boss man there, Ketchum, is hirin' men.'

Kate gave the stranger a longer look. It awakened long ago memories. A bank raid in Kansas that turned into a wild, bloody shoot-out between the law and the would-be bank robbers, sending the citizens of Newton scattering for cover. When the shooting stopped, five of the raiders and two deputies lay dead in the street. From the cathouse porch she and the rest of the girls saw the only raider still alive being part dragged, part carried to the jailhouse, and by the way he looked he seemed badly wounded. Badly wounded or not, Kate knew she was gazing at the same man.

'I've seen you once before, mister,' she said, hard-voiced. 'Long time back, Kansas way, trying to rob a bank. You got yourself all shot to hell, I didn't think much of your chances of pulling through.' She brought the shotgun up sharply. 'You'll have no chance at all of getting back up on a horse again if you think you've stumbled across some easy pickin's here.'

Sam thin-smiled. 'I can't recollect seein' you in Newton, ma'am,' he said. 'Though at the time I was in no fit state to notice what was goin' on around me. I was tryin' to stop myself from dyin'. And I ain't come across the crick to rob you, ma'am. I've just finished a ten-year stretch in the State Pen, I've no hankerin' to go back inside again. If you can't help me out I'll dismount and walk the rest of the way to the Double Star. I'm told if I follow the crick I'll come on to it.'

In the profession she had followed as a girl, Kate was expert in judging men's moods and intentions, in and out of bed, and she could see no signs of deceit in the all-bone face. She believed what he had told her, that he wouldn't do her any hurt. And it was a long walk to the Double Star ranch.

'Step down, mister,' she said. 'And have a look in the barn. There ought to be a tool of sorts you can use lying about in there. While you're doing that I'll heat up the coffee; you're welcome to partake in a cup.' Kate smiled to herself. It was true, the saying that whores had hearts of gold, she thought.

Sam touched the brim of his hat. 'Why, thank you, ma'am,' he said. He grinned at Kate as he swung down from his mount. 'I'd welcome stretchin' my legs. I ain't quite got my saddle butt yet.'

While in the barn seeing to his horse's hoof, Sam got to wondering where the man of the house was. Surely, he thought, the woman, and not an uncomely-looking one, wouldn't be living in this backwoods territory on her own? He reckoned her husband must be out ploughing, or checking on the stock he ran on the place. And why had she moved here from Kansas?

'Horse,' he said, 'why the heck am I wonderin' about some folks I ain't goin' to be seein' for no more than it takes to down a cup of coffee, and will never clap eyes on again when I've got a whole heap of thinkin' to do for myself? The only things I've done in my life is to heist stages and rob banks and I ain't been over successful doin' that. How the hell will I fare doin' ranch chores bein' I ain't no cow hand and you sure ain't no cow pony.'

He lowered the stone-cleared hoof to the ground. 'It still could be a mite tender, but if we take it easy we oughta be able to make it to the Double Star with me sittin' in the saddle. You stay here and rest that foot while I go and sample some of that kindly woman's coffee.'

Kate had made the coffee and was looking in the mirror, tying back her hair from her face, smoothing down the faded print dress she had changed into. Old habits died hard, she thought wryly. Even if it wasn't some high-rolling client but an ex-jailbird-come-saddle-bum having a cup of coffee before she sent him on his way.

Though she did worry about her guest's business with the Double Star ranch.

On her weekly visits to Spine Ridge for supplies, the talk among the men in the town was why Silas Ketchum, boss of the Double Star, was doing a lot of hiring for the size of the spread he owned. And the newly hired hands weren't the regular dollar-a-day-all-found cow herders, but men who had the chip-on-the-shoulder look of men more familiar with the use of guns than the nursing of longhorns.

For what purpose? That unanswered question chewed away at the insides of the owners of the holdings scattered along White Water creek. There had been no Indian trouble or cattle-lifting activities in the territory to justify

Ketchum's practically doubling the size of his crew. But the sodbusters knew that the biggest problem a rancher faced was having a regular supply of good grass and sweet water for his cows, expecially if he was intending to enlarge his herd.

Ketchum's eyes could be casting envious eyes at their water, and how much grass could be grown on the land they had planted with corn and vegetables? The uneasy living together of sodbusters and cattlemen in this section of the Nations could soon be coming to a close, ending up with blood being spilt, theirs and their families.

If that sort of trouble was about to break out, Kate opined, it would be well for her to have her few belongings packed ready for a quick getaway. She wanted no part in a goddamned range war. A lone woman, armed with only a shotgun, couldn't stand off a bunch of torch-bearing night riders coming in to burn her out. Or stop a herd of stampeding longhorns turning her growing land into a dust bowl.

Kate gave a dry, mirthless laugh. And she was tarting herself up and offering a cup of coffee to a man who could be paying her a night-time call. Her new life had already turned sour on her; the man whose name she had taken to stop the church-going females in town treating her as a scarlet woman, had died of a sudden heart attack. Being full growing season, it hadn't been too much of a struggle to feed herself and the few cattle and horses she owned, but ploughing and the gathering in of the winter feed were tasks she couldn't face.

She would have to sell up and head back to Newton and take up being a working girl again in the cathouse. That's if she could find a man foolish enough to buy the place knowing that he could soon lose it to a big rancher. Her leaving the cathouse to take up the life of a sodbuster's woman was beginning to look like a bad move on her part. Kate gave another cynical laugh. What the hell did she expect from a whirlwind courtship? And courtships didn't come any faster, even in eastern published romance stories, And she wasn't really a widow. Her union with Mr Fischer hadn't been blessed by a preacher.

Madame Carla, the owner of the sporting house, had come into the parlour where she and the rest of the girls were getting themselves ready for a busy night being it was payday at the local ranches, with the unusual news that an elderly German sodbuster drinking in the Plains View saloon was telling all in earshot that he was seeking a woman to cook for him and keep house on his new farm in the Nations. Marry her if a suitable female came forward. Seemingly the farmer's wife had died of smallpox when that fearful scourge struck the migrant wagon train just after leaving Independence, Missouri.

'I know you girls sometime moan

about the rough ways of some of the assholes of ranch hands you entertain,' Madame Carla had said. 'But it's an easier life than working for some old German sodbuster trying to scratch a living on a dirt farm. Fixing his vittals for him, mending and washing his drawers, m'be spelling him behind the plough. Not forgetting, sharing his bed regular like.'

Kate mulled over the idea of being an elderly sodbuster's wife, housekeeper, whatever. Having been raised on a Missouri dirt farm she knew she would be living in a draughty, roof-leaking shack and how heavy the workload would be. And the old sodbuster could turn out to be a smelly old goat. Though he wouldn't be any more stinking, or randy than some of the cow hands who paid for her favours. At least, Kate thought, if she took up the old German's offer, and he accepted it, she would have a place of her own, working for herself.

Madame Carla would hoof her out

once she was too old to be profitable to her. Kate shuddered. She could end up in some dive of a border *cantina* entertaining clients whose manners and hygiene were only one step up from a hog's. What the hell, Kate thought, what was she losing leaving the cathouse? Unseen by Madame Carla or any of the girls, she sneaked out of the back entrance.

Kate didn't go into the saloon, not wanting the drinkers, some of them clients of hers, cat-calling and hooting at her as she spoke to the farmer. She had heard tell that many of the German immigrants were strict hellfire and damnation Christians and would no more hire a well-soiled dove as a housekeeper than sit down and sup with the Devil.

She waited patiently in the shadow of the store porch across the street from the saloon until she saw a stoop-backed elderly man dressed in a store suit come out of the saloon and begin walking across the Kansas–Topeka railroad track towards the livery barn. A man who, Kate opined, could only be the woman-seeking farmer.

She caught up with him as he reached the tarp-covered wagon the sides and tailgate of which were festooned with pots, pans and digging tools and didn't waste any time putting her proposition to him. Some of the other girls could also be thinking it was time to give some thought to security in their middle age. And whores aged fast.

'I ain't willing to marry you, mister,' she said. 'But I am willing to keep house for you, and work your land with you.'

Karl Fischer swung round, eyes widening in surprise and disbelief. The girl was young enough to be his daughter and pretty-looking as well. She must be joshing, he thought. The drinkers at the bar must have put her up to it and waited for their derisive laughter from the shadows as she tried to make a fool of him.

Kate seeing the look of uncertainty

on the old man's face guessed, wrongly, that he didn't think her capable of helping him to run a farm. 'I was raised on a farm in Missouri,' she said, defensively. 'I was taught two chores; Ma taught me to cook and Pa taught me to work the soil.'

Karl favoured the girl with a shrewd-eyed look, liking what he saw and heard. She would know working on a farm wasn't like working in some general store. Though she had to go through a final test to prove her offer was genuine.

'I'll be leaving for the Nations as soon as I hitch the mules to the wagon, miss,' he said. 'Will you be ready to ride with me?'

Kate was rapidly doing her own weighing up. She could be jumping out of a griddle into one hell of a hot fire. The old German could be a woman-beater, a whiskey-soak, and there would only be the two of them living nose to nose in a shack in the back of the beyond in the lawless land of the

Nations. But all she could see in the German's face was what she had remembered seeing in her pa's eyes, the weariness of a man shouldering a whole heap of worry and anguish. Even if she was wrong in her reading of him, she had handled rougher, younger men than the old sodbuster.

Kate smiled. 'Mister,' she said, 'what I've got in this world to pack I'll be back before you can get the mules outa that barn.'

That had been five years ago and until now Kate had never regretted taking up with Karl Fischer. It had been hard work helping him to build up the farm from a piece of backwoods' wilderness yet it had given her a sense of belonging she had never had as a good-time girl.

Karl hadn't turned out to be a smelly old goat or a woman-beater or drunkard but a kind, gentle-mannered man and had wanted to marry her, an offer she turned down, albeit reluctantly, still wishing to hold on to her new-found independence. Though she did, willingly, share his bed. And not wanting to be branded by the God-fearing womenfolk of Spine Ridge as a harlot, she called herself Mrs Fischer.

Then six months ago her 'husband' had died of a heart attack and Kate was burdened with worries. Mr Fischer had given her a future, could she, on her own, hang on to it? If the rumours were right, Ketchum of the Double Star and his grasping need for grass and water would make it harder for her to do so. Kate ceased her ruminating when she heard footsteps on the porch, though still feeling anger and frustation at the possibility of losing all that Karl and she had built up with the sweat of honest, seemingly endless days of labour.

She had quickly assessed that the gaunt-faced, ex-jailbird meant her no harm. At least he was someone to talk to for a brief spell, making a change to the farm's critters with whom she had been having a one-sided conversation since Karl's death. She got up from the chair and opened the door and invited her visitor inside.

Sam was surprised at the sodbuster's wife asking him into her home, considering only a while back she was all set to pepper him with a couple of loads of buckshot. And yet here he was sitting at her table, with her and a steaming jug of coffee and plate of freshly baked cookies in front of him. It felt as though he was sitting in some city coffee house.

It was a neat, well-kept room, a room the farmer and his wife had obviously taken pride in. He had spent most of his adult life in ramshackle cabins or mountain caves. Though it puzzled him that he could see no signs of a man's presence in the shack. No spare pair of boots on the porch, no heavy-weather gear hanging on the door. And no signs of the mess kids make.

Sam didn't want to be nosy but after ten years in the State Pen he had a strong hankering to have a spell of small-talking with a female, hear a woman's soft-toned voice again.

Casually he said, 'It ain't no business of mine, ma'am, and I hope you'll not be offended by me askin', but I can't see any signs of the man of the house, or a family for that matter. Surely you ain't been runnin' this place on your own?'

The look Sam got back from Kate had him pondering again. It was a steely-eyed look of a woman who had taken some hard knocks in her life and had ridden them out. The hard times he was thinking about had nothing to do with all the hassle and worry running a farm heaps on folk. But as he had just said it was no business of his to ask her what the troubles had been.

'I have no family, and no husband,' replied Kate. 'My man died a few months back. But I reckon you'll find out all about me and the other farmers along the creek from your new boss at the Double Star.' Kate's face hardened. She suddenly didn't have the urge to pass the time of day with her visitor, or she would tell him that as a bank-robber and jailbird he would fit in well with the gunslinging sons-of-bitches Ketchum was hiring to drive the settlers off their holdings.

'Drink your coffee, before it gets cold, mister,' she snapped. 'I've got to feed my stock. As you can figure it isn't easy for a widow to run a farm on her own. Especially when there's the likelihood of some big operator taking it from you.' Kate got to her feet and walked out into the kitchen, and a gaping-mouthed Sam at the sudden change in the widow's attitude towards him, heard the back door bang shut.

What the hell had upset her? he thought wildly. She had invited him to her table, then, within a couple of minutes she had given him the fish-eyed look and stormed out. It wasn't that she hadn't known she was sitting down with an ex-owlhoot and a man who had done time in the State Pen. It could be, he reasoned, that she was still more than a mite touchy about losing her husband and having to shoulder all the chores on the farm. Not to mention the fella who she said wanted to take over all the farms along the creek. His boss? For crying out loud he wasn't even on the Double Star payroll! All this wondering was turning him dizzy.

Sam knew two things for sure: the widow, for her own personal reasons wanted him off her land, pronto, and why was no business of his. In two scalding mouthfuls he finished off his coffee, then left the shack and climbed on to his mount.

'Friend,' he said to his horse. 'That was the shortest conversation I've ever had with a female. That fine-lookin' widow lady is nursin' one helluva problem. I was lucky not to get a coupla barrels of shotgun lead in my hide instead of the coffee.'

He cast a final over-the-shoulder glance at the shack as he crossed the creek to get back on to the main trail, but could see no sign of the widow. Then he got to wondering what she knew about the activities of his new boss — that's if Ketchum ever became his boss — that was so upsetting to her. More importantly, would, whatever his 'boss' was up to, be upsetting to him?

From the side of the shack, Kate watched her visitor ride away, wondering, as he must be, she thought, about her sudden change of heart towards him. She had wanted to sit at the table for a few minutes' chat, but an unexpected flare of anger within her stopped her from doing so. Slowly, Kate was beginning to understand her flare of anger.

It was, she opined, the natural reaction of someone not prepared to sit back and do damn all when a taking man craved for her farm. No land-grabbing son-of-a-bitch was going to steal all that she and Karl had sweated for. If she didn't make a stand, Karl wouldn't rest in his grave. And she wasn't going to take the easy road out by selling her land to one of the farmers along the creek.

Kate's lips thinned as the trail dust of her visitor drifted away into a faint brown haze. 'Mister,' she murmured, 'you seem a nice enough fella for a bank robber, but you won't be welcome to step on my porch again.'

Then, as she walked back into the shack, cold logic thinking took over and Kate began to shiver as she realized just how big of a hell she could have raised for herself by her mule-headed stubbornness.

2

Before the trail forked, one leg cutting away eastwards from the creek leading towards a smudge of buildings of a small township on the skyline, Sam saw a flatbed wagon heading in his direction. As it came nearer he could see it was being driven by a young boy, with a much younger girl sitting beside him. He edged his horse off to the left of the narrow trail to allow the wagon right of passage, smiling and touching his hat in the time-honoured meeting-on-the-trail gesture. Sam's 'Howdy' died in his throat. Ten years ago, the look of pure hate the boy had cast him would have earned him a pistol-whipping, or a slug in his hide just to show him to mind his manners.

The boy must have applied the whip to the horse because the wagon picked up speed fast, covering him and his mount in a choking dust cloud. What sort of territory was he riding into, Sam wondered? He had only met three people and all of them showed that they hated his guts. The widow woman may not have been friendly towards him knowing that he had once been a bank robber and an ex-con, but the kids in the wagon didn't know him from Adam. There and then Sam decided that if he didn't get on the Double Star payroll he would ride south into Texas and see if he could strike more friendlier folk.

About two miles further along the creek, Sam saw the first of several herds of grazing longhorns and beyond them the squat shapes of ranch buildings. He kneed his horse into a ground-eating trot, keen to find out if the unfriendliness he had met on the trail reached as far as the Double Star.

The big house, a long, rambling timber-built structure, stood on the crest of a slight rise. The owner, Sam thought, would get great satisfaction sitting on his front porch viewing, unhindered, across all the land he owned and his stock of cows roaming over it.

Before riding up the grade to the ranch house, Sam passed two groups of men. The bunch on the creek side of the trail were regular ranch-hands busy branding several mavericks, Sam catching the tangy stench of singed hair and burnt hide. The five men chatting and smoking outside what he took to be the bunkhouse hadn't the cut of workaday cow men. They were shut-faced, cold-staring men, all sporting pistols, some two, sheathed about their bellies in well-filled shellbelts. So what, Sam thought, momentarily, even hard men have to take up honest work in order to eat. Though that reasoning didn't stop his nerves from twitching. Something didn't smell quite right about the crew of the Double Star.

When another man came out of the bunkhouse similarly pistolled up, Sam knew in an instant his nerves hadn't played him false. The pinch-assed-faced son-of-a-bitch was Dan Morrow and had once ridden with the Butler gang. Cal Butler, not backward in gunning down anyone who stood between him and the cash he was after, couldn't stomach needless killings on a raid and had told him to quit the gang or he'd string him up and claim the reward on his head. Morrow, like him, had never done an honest day's work in his adult life, though now, it seemed, he'd had to try suchlike chores, but Morrow would sooner kill his grandpa and steal what he had than raise an ounce of honest sweat. Morrow gave him a sneering look as he rode by him.

It was easy to figure the widow's statement of how he would find out all about her and the rest of the farmers along the creek from the boss of the Double Star, know of Ketchum's tactics to drive them off their lands. He understood now the kid with the wagon and his drop-dead glare. In his eyes, he was just another one of the Double

Star's hired guns.

Sam cursed; he had hard-assed it all the way here for damn all; he wasn't about to get himself involved in a range war. He drew his horse's head round to ride off Double Star land to seek more peaceful employment elsewhere. Maybe tending woollies. Anything as long as it didn't call on him to use his guns.

'Are you looking for work?' the call from the smaller of the two men who had stepped out on to the porch of the big house stayed his hand.

The man who had spoken was a small but stocky-built man wearing a yellow duster over a well-cut store suit and a wide-brimmed, white Plains hat. He had the fixed stone-hard look of a man used to making men jump to his tune, a man who smiled rarely. Sam tagged the little Jim Dandy as Ketchum, boss man of the ranch. The other man, much bigger in all ways, who was wearing normal range clothes and favouring him with a fish-eyed look, must be the straw boss. Sam nudged his horse closer to the porch.

'I was, mister,' he said, leaning easily across his saddle horn. 'I was willin' to tend your cows, m'be rob a bank for you if my cut was big enough,' he said, in a matter-of-fact voice. 'But I ain't doin' any night ridin' against some poor sodbusters with that back-shootin' asshole Mr Morrow there, and the scum standin' alongside him. I ain't sunk that low yet.'

Sam saw the straw boss's face mottle red in anger and his hand drop down to the pistol belted across his fat-gutted stomach.

'Don't even consider it, pilgrim,' he said, straightening up, his voice as hard as his face. 'Or so help me I'll shoot you dead.'

'Are you that fast with a gun you can take all of us?' Silas Ketchum grated, gimlet-eying the man who was insulting him on his own porch.

Sam favoured him with a wolfish grin and in a flash of movement a long barrelled .44 Colt was fisted and cocked and covering the pair. 'I'm fast enough to put you and that straw boss of yours past bein' interested in what happens to me.'

The big straw boss began to dirty-mouth Sam, but Sam noticed he kept his hand clear of his gun. He risked a quick glance over his shoulder at Morrow and the other hired guns to see if they had noticed that a Mexican standoff was taking place in front of their noses. For all his bold-assed stance and words, Sam knew he would never ride past them alive if they sensed he was holding the man who paid their wages at gunpoint.

Sam cursed. His goddamned pride had placed him between a rock and a definite hard place. Surprisingly it was Ketchum who got him out of it.

The rancher stepped right up to the porch rails and fish-eyed Sam. 'Mister,' he said, 'being I'm in a kindly mood I'll give you a choice: you can either get off my land pronto, or I'll get my men to gun you down. What's it to be?'

Sam had to admit the little rancher had balls in taking over the situation. Then again he ought to have known that a man who was contemplating starting a range war and all the mayhem that could raise would be no chicken-livered store clerk. And Sam was also a man who heeded good advice when needed, whoever it came from. Still holding his pistol he dug his heels into his mount's ribs, hard, sending it off in a squealing, protesting, high-kicking gallop, his legs brushing the side of the house as he cornered it.

A hundred or so yards beyond the house without being fired on, he sheathed his pistol, but still gave his horse its head. He began to breathe more easily when he saw no signs of any pursuers though thinking that he hadn't made a good impression on the people he had met since riding into the Nations.

Ketchum, face etched in hard lines of barely controlled anger, turned to his straw boss. 'Go across to Morrow,

Jackson,' he said. 'He knows that blowhard sonuvabitch. Tell him to have the 'breed ride with him and hunt him down. Promise them a bonus if they bring the bastard back alive so I have the pleasure of hanging him on the big tree.' The rancher smiled icily. 'When they get back we'll start showing those stinking sodbusters that their days of spoiling good grazing grass are over.'

3

Sam opined he was clear of the Double Star range and with no sign of riders hammering along his back trail he eased up on his near panicky dash. In the distance he could see a range of jagged, crested hills. Somewhere along the foot of them he judged he would find a hole-up for the night. Eat, then, consider the explosive situation in this part of the Nations and his uneasy feeling that Mr Silas Ketchum wouldn't take it lightly him spitting in his eye, if it was wiser to quit the Nations and head for Texas and find work on some ranch there. Surely, he thought, he couldn't get a colder reception in the Lone Star State than he'd had here.

★ ★ ★

'He's headin' west, Morrow,' the 'breed Sal, said after a quick, but all-seeing glance at the trail. 'He's makin' for Spine Ridge, but it'll be dark soon and he'll not want to risk his or his mount's neck ridin' across territory he don't know at night. I reckon he'll make camp in the hills.' The 'breed's face twitched in what Dan Morrow guessed to be a part-Indian smile. It frightened the crap out of him, and he wasn't a man who scared easily. 'That bonus the boss promised us if we bring in the sonuvabitch alive,' the 'breed continued, 'is as good as in our hands.'

Morrow had been led to believe that the 'breed was a good tracker, but he couldn't see even a full-blood Apache finding a one man camp in the tangle of canyons and draws of the Spine Ridge hills. Though he didn't tell the 'breed that they would be losing a night's sleep on a hopeless task, not wanting to see the 'breed's bad side. Instead he just said, 'How?' and favoured his partner with a puzzled look.

'Easy,' replied the 'breed. 'The trail your one-time pard will take when he breaks camp swings round the far edge of the hills, a long ride. I know a way through that high ground that — '

'That oughta get us hunkered down behind some brush or rock waiting for him to ride on to our guns,' interrupted Morrow. His smile held a mite more warmth than the 'breed's had. 'You're right, Sal, that bonus is as good as ours. Let's go and find that cut through.'

4

Come dawn, Sam had made up his mind regarding his future. He would ride south and try his luck in Texas. As short as his stay in the Nations had been he'd had his bellyful of it, with or without a possible range war breaking out. Though that decision presented him with a problem. He couldn't just point his horse's nose south where he knew the Texas border was and rib-kick it into stepping out along the trail. There could be obstacles such as deep canyons, high mountains, fast-flowing rivers and maybe scalp-hunting broncos barring his way, forcing him to double back for days before once again he was heading south. And he would be only carrying enough supplies his horse could comfortably bear and wouldn't be able to bank on riding into some town, or coming across a sutler's store to replenish his supplies.

His best bet, Sam reasoned, was to follow this trail; wagons as well as riders used it, so it should lead to a town or settlement. Then he would try and buy a cheap pack horse and load it up with supplies, then ask in what direction the nearest Texas/Kansas cattle trail lay. The main cow trails leading to the railhead cattle towns in Kansas were as wide as the Missouri river and even a half-blind Eastern dude couldn't miss hitting Texas following a suchlike path.

By noon, Sam was rounding the western end of the hills, riding relaxed and easy, ignorant of the danger he was riding into until he felt a searing pain rip across his right shoulder. He heard the crack of the rifle that had fired the shot as he flung himself sideways out of his saddle to land heavily on the ground that caused him to gasp out loud in agony and scramble frantically for the shelter of a shale and rock tumble. He managed a fearsome rictus-like smile. The coldness of his reception in the territory had sure hotted up.

Sam did some rapid thinking. If he hadn't been swaying half asleep in his saddle he would have had a busted shoulder instead of a knife slash of a wound across his upper arm. Another thing he was certain of, whoever it was had plugged him had shot to wound not to kill. He had been an easy target for a killing head shot. Someone wanted to take him alive, disable him, knock the fighting out of him.

It didn't take Sam long to figure out who that would be: rancher Ketchum, as he had guessed, was a man who nursed a grudge. Now he had to come up with a quick plan for him to get the better of the bushwhackers, two, at least, he thought, unless he wanted to find out just how hard Ketchum held grudges.

Sam's face twisted into a savage scowl. The rancher wasn't the only one who couldn't swallow being slighted. The son-of-a-bitch had more than slighted him, he had drawn blood.

Being raised in the hill country of Missouri, where even an unkindly look would have whole families shooting at each other, it came natural to Sam to want blood in return. Ketchum would soon discover he was fighting two wars, his and the sodbusters'. Sam's death's-head smile returned. It gave him something to occupy his time; he would never have made it as a ranch-hand here or in Texas. Though before he could start getting even with Ketchum he had to first outwit the bushwhackers who shouldn't be long in breaking their cover.

'Keep a watchful eye on the sonuvabitch, Sal,' Morrow warned. 'I've winged him sorely, but the day the law wiped out the Butler gang, Hetheridge took four shells in his hide before he was brought down.'

'Let's hope then he ain't as tough as he was,' replied Sal. 'I'd hate havin' to kill him and lose out in collectin' Ketchum's bonus.'

The pair of them were walking

cautiously along the trail towards the rock fall, holding pistols now for close-quarter shooting. And just as wary-eyed, Sam, sitting with his back up against a rock watched them closing in on him. He gave a grunt of satisfaction. He had surmised right, there were only two of them: one of them the trigger-happy Morrow, the other by his hard-angled face, a mixed-blood man. He would be the man to down first if his hoped-for break came. Sending Morrow to hell to meet up with Cal Butler and the rest of the boys would give him great pleasure.

Sam knew that his hoped-for break, miracle more likely, he soberly thought, depended on his believing the ambushers had really only meant to wound him and not some bad shooting on their part. Those doubts were soon to be resolved one way or another.

Morrow grinned at the sight of Sam's pain-racked face and him clutching at his wounded shoulder with his left hand. He held his pistol loosely on him.

'You ain't about to cause me and my pard any trouble, are you, Sam? It ain't no extra sweat for me to haul you back to the Double Star wrapped up neat and tidy like in a sheet of tarp slung across your horse's ass.'

Sam fierce-eyed the pair of them. 'If you bastards hadn't smashed up my shoulder and I hadn't lost my gun when you knocked me outa the saddle, then by hell, Morrow, you'd have had a fight on your hands!'

The 'breed's gaze flickered downwards, taking in the empty holster then back on to Sam's face again as if trying to read his mind. Sam did some silent cursing. The suspicious-minded son-of-a-bitch had to fall for his way-out ploy, or he had to resign himself to swinging on Ketchum's hanging tree. It was Morrow who gave him the prayed-for break.

Morrow's grin widened. 'He ain't goin' to cause us any bother, Sal,' he said. 'His fightin' back days are over. Bring up the horses then we can go and make Mr Ketchum's day.'

The 'breed gave Sam one last poker-faced look, slipped his pistol back into its holster then set off back along the trail to the horses. A still grinning Morrow turned to watch him go and for a few seconds his gun swung away from Sam. It wasn't much of a break but it was all he could hope for. In one swift movement his left hand slipped off his wounded shoulder and reached under his coat. When Morrow faced him again he saw that Sam had not lost his pistol, and he was too late to do anything about it but lose his smile and die. Sam's single shot killed him before the force of the discharge flung him backwards to the ground.

The 'breed proved Sam's estimation of him being the more dangerous of the pair by his Indian blood giving him quicker reactions when in danger. He had whirled round, pistol in his hand before Sam pulled off his second shot. The two pistol shots echoed each other, the 'breed's shell, aimed and fired more hastily, chipped splinters off the rock Sam was sitting against, drawing blood from his right cheek.

Sam's shot hammered into the 'breed's chest tearing its killing way through his heart. Sal's face screwed up in fearsome agony as he folded at the knees. His fast dying reflexes fired off another pistol-load harmlessly into the dirt at his feet before the gun dropped out of his hand as he sank to the ground.

A stone-faced Sam watched him crumple to the ground and lie there unmoving. Sam had seen many dead men, some by his own hand, and the 'breed looked dead to him, there was no need to kill him twice over, shells cost money. He got to his feet and looked along the trail to see if there were any more ambushers hanging around. He gave a deep sigh of relief when all he could see was the dead men's horses. His trick wouldn't work twice; he was damned lucky it had worked at all.

Slowly, thoughtfully, he eased the hammer of the Colt forward and stuffed it into the waistband of his pants handy for a left-hand cross draw, and then decided it was getting-to-hell-out-of-it time, but fast. If any rider came along he would have some hard explaining to do and if it became known he had been a member of the notorious Cal Butler gang, his version of the shoot-out wouldn't go well at all for him.

Groaning with pain, he managed to heave Morrow and the 'breed's bodies on to their horses. He slapped the mounts' flanks which sent them trotting with their grisly loads in the general direction of the Double Star range. He had spat in Ketchum's eye with some vengeance, so from now on, if he wanted to stay alive, he would have to sleep lightly with a cocked pistol in his hand. That didn't worry Sam unduly. He had been giving the slip to marshals' posses for years; men expert in tracking down men posted on Wanted flyers. A bunch of ranch-hands and a few hired guns shouldn't prove too hard to dodge if he kept his wits about him, especially if they were busy harassing the sodbusters at the same time. And there was the good chance Ketchum would think he had ass-kicked it out of the Nations and would forget about him. That should win him the time to get himself familiar with the territory and when the edge came his way show Mr 'Almighty' Silas Ketchum how a Missouri country boy can cut him down to size.

What did worry Sam was his wounded arm and the rock splash cuts on his face. The wounds, though painful, weren't very deep but could go bad on him if not treated. Cleaning up his face was no problem but his arm wound was too high for him to bandage it single-handedly and was bleeding heavily, seeping through his shirt and jacket. He couldn't ride into a town and ask the local doctor to treat his wounds. Awkward questions could be asked how he came by them. If it was already known in town about Morrow and the 'breed, his shot-up appearance would link him with the killings and he would be handing himself to Ketchum on a plate.

Maybe, Sam thought, as he climbed on to his horse, the feisty widow lady would clean up his wounds, after all they were now on the same side. Though he didn't want to hamper what action he might take against Ketchum by allying himself with a bunch of hoe-toting sodbusters. Sam grinned. More than likely the widow would put a few more holes in his hide with her shotgun and save Ketchum a job. He could but hope, he opined, giving his horse its head. He cut away from the main trail, heading for the creek across open country. He would have to ride carefully at all times, so he might as well get into the swing of it straight away.

★ ★ ★

Sam forded the creek longways before the point he had crossed it the first time he had called on the widow, then dismounting, approached the shack from the rear, rein leading his mount and sheltered most of the way by a line of fully leafed trees. Closer to the shack, Sam looped the reins over a handy branch and continued on foot, hawk-eyeing the back door, face fixed in a nervous grimace, expecting at any moment to see the door swing open and the widow standing there, shotgun blazing.

It was more gut chewing than robbing a bank, Sam thought. On a raid he could fire back if being shot at, he didn't know if he could cut loose at a shotgun-wielding widow intent on doing him serious harm.

Almost at the door, he heard the snorting and restless shuffling of the feet of a horse. Risking a look round the corner of the shack, Sam saw what he took to be a saddled-up plough horse tethered to one of the front porch posts. Sam cursed, the widow had a visitor. He now had two to stop from pulling guns on him before he could explain he hadn't been taken on as a hired gun by Ketchum.

He drew his pistol and slowly lifted the door latch and stood hesitantly on the threshold for a moment or two, like some greenhorn drummer nervous about selling his wares, before stepping inside. He heard the mutter of voices coming from the living-room and, as he strode, cat-footed, to the living-room door, he caught a glimpse of his dust and blood-caked face in a mirror hanging on the wall. His own mother, Sam thought wryly, would shoot him on sighting such a fearsome mask of a face. That and the drawn gun ought to give him the threatening edge when he confronted the widow and her visitor.

'Pa says it's safer for you to come and stay at our place, Mrs Fischer,' Jem Douglas said. 'Leastways at night. All the families along the creek are expecting trouble from Ketchum soon. And you bein' a widow lady, livin' on your own, your place could be the first farm the sonsuvbitches hit.'

Kate's reply was a gasped, 'Holy Mother!' as she gazed wide-eyed at her earlier visitor coming into the room, fierce-faced and holding a gun.

A startled Jem spun round trying to bring the small-bore squirrel gun he held on to Sam. Sam recognized him as the kid driving the wagon on the trail who had given him a drop-dead glare. 'Just don't go off at half-cock, boy,' he said, pressing the muzzle of his Colt hard up against Jem's head. 'Hear me out first.'

'What is there to talk about to a hired killer?' Jem said, more defiantly than he felt, eyeballing the Colt pistol held by a man he guessed would use it if he so much as broke wind. 'We won't sell our land to your boss no matter what trouble he siccs on to us. It's our land and we farmers intend to stay and fight to hold on to it!'

Kate couldn't trust herself to speak. What did the hired gun mean he had come here to talk, she thought wildly, when he had burst in on them with his pistol cocked and face all bloody-streaked like some Comanche buck painted up for war. He had come to burn her out on Ketchum's orders as Jem's pa had said. Her fears reached every part of her body. Finally she managed to say, hoarse-voiced, 'What do you mean, talk? How can I believe you just mean to have words with us when you have come, uninvited, into my living-room threatening us with a cocked pistol?'

'I had to come in fast and threat-enin', ma'am,' replied Sam. 'So you couldn't use that shotgun on me.' Sam smiled. 'Like you 'threatened' to do if I ever called on you again. And the state of my ugly mug and the wound on my arm is what I'm here to talk about.' Then he told them how he had been bushwhacked. 'I was lucky,' he said. 'The two fellas Ketchum sent to kill me weren't so fortunate; they're dead. I figure Ketchum will be as mad as hell when he finds out he's lost two of his crew and his bull-headed pride could have him sendin' more of his men to put paid to me so I have to keep clear of any town bein' I don't know who Ketchum's friends are. I ain't about to aid Ketchum in killin' me.' He gave another grin. 'So here I am, ma'am, on the wild chance you'll clean up my wounds, bein' we're on the same side in this forthcomin' shindig.'

Kate's tensed-up nerves began to unwind. Her earlier assessment of the stranger had been proved right. He might have been a notorious bank robber, but as mean-looking as he was he wasn't a fork-tongued talker. He hadn't come here to do Ketchum's work. 'Take your coat off, mister, er, and sit yourself down,' she said, 'while I'll get water boiled up. I'm Kate Fischer, by the way, and this is Jem Douglas, son of my nearest neighbour.'

'I'm Sam Hethridge,' Sam replied, as

he removed his coat painfully and sat down.

'Are you goin' to fight alongside us farmers, Mr Hethridge? Jem asked eagerly.

Sam shook his head. 'You farmers can act all legal like in your fight with Ketchum,' he said. 'Send a delegation up to the state capital complainin' that some land-grabbin' rancher is tryin' to steal the land you hold rights to.' Sam bared his teeth in a fearsome smile that froze Jem's blood. He was glad he had listened to his sister's advice not to draw his gun on Mr Hethridge when they had met him on the trail or he would be lying in a pine box under six feet of dirt and rocks by now. 'My disgreement with Mr Ketchum is more personal,' continued Sam. 'A kinda blood-for-blood situation. It's better you farmers ain't linked to a fella who could get strung up for murder.'

A slack-jawed Jem looked at Sam hardly taking in what had been so casually said. Was Mr Hethridge joshing him when he talked about ranging a one-man vendetta against the Double Star? He could see no signs of humour in the ice-cold eyes set deep in a blood-encrusted face.

Kate came back into the room with a bundle of cloths draped over one arm and carrying a bowl of steaming hot water. 'I'll see to your arm first, Mr Hethridge,' she said. 'It's still bleeding a little. And you go back home, Jem, and thank your pa for worrying about me, but tell him I'm staying here.' Kate's face hardened in unyielding lines. 'If Ketchum wants my land he'll have to drag me off it kicking and screaming.'

Jem said his goodbyes to leave Mrs Fischer to dress Mr Hethridge's wounds. He had something else to tell his pa; the fight against Ketchum had already started and the first encounter had been in their favour.

★ ★ ★

'There,' said Kate, straightening up. 'You look a little more human now your face is cleaned up. But I wouldn't shave for a while, or you'll open up the cuts again. Your arm should be OK, m'be a little stiff for a day or two, but it's a clean wound. I've a shirt and a jacket belonging to my late husband that should fit you.' She smiled slightly. 'You don't want to be seen riding with bloodstained clothes on. I'll cook you a hot meal, Mr Hethridge, then you can rest up here for the night.' The smile played about her lips again. 'To kinda make up for clearing you off my porch with a shotgun.'

Sam smiled back at her as he slipped his coat back on. There was nothing he would like better than to spend the night with a fine-looking widow lady but it couldn't be. Life or death moves, *his* life or death, had to be made. Pleasurable times were possible future hopes, if he ever got a future. 'I'll have that meal. I can't remember the last time I sat at a table eating a home-cooked meal, but as I told the boy if Ketchum gets to know that the sodbu — , beggin' your pardon, ma'am, the farmers, are feeding the killer of two of his men, it will give him one helluva excuse to come down hard on you all, with the law backin' him up.'

★   ★   ★

A well-fed, smiling Sam rode out when it was fully dark. A gunnysack of rations for him and his horse was hooked across the pommel of his saddle. He had the promise from Mrs Fischer that she would pass the word around to the other farmers to expect him to call on any of them when he ran out of food.

'It will keep you out of Spine Ridge, Mr Hethridge,' she had said. Then she smiled. 'We sodbusters owe you at least that much help.' Then, as though it was the natural thing to do, she reached up and kissed him.

Sam's grin was still showing as his horse splashed its way across the creek, still feeling the warm soft lips on his cheek. He gave a deep nostalgic smile. As well as being a long time since he partook of a home-cooked meal it had been just as long since a woman had planted a kiss on him, for free. By the time he had cleared the widow's land, his smile had gone. Acting like a lovesick kid was the surest way to get himself killed.

Kate watched him go with far more tender feelings than she'd had towards him on his first visit. 'Mr Hethridge,' she said softly, 'Fate has sure dealt you one helluva bum hand. You haven't been more than a few weeks out of the Pen and you could be heading back there again, never to come out, or get real lucky and get yourself shot dead.'

Kate turned and walked back into the house dabbing at her eyes that had suddenly become moist with the back of her hands. 'You come back here, Mr Hethridge,' she said, still in the same low-toned voice. 'And spend the night in my bed.' Then firm-voiced, she added, 'And to hell with Ketchum and his war!'

* * *

Ketchum, standing on his porch, listened impassively to his straw boss telling him about the killing of the two men whom he had trusted to bring him the son-of-a-bitch who had had the gall to draw a gun on him, standing, goddamn it, on his own stoop.

'The men with the supply wagon ran into the horses with the bodies slung across their backs halfway along the trail to Spine Ridge,' Jackson said. 'Figurin' you'll want to know, urgent like, about the shootin', one of them rode back here with the news. The other two crew with the wagon are buryin' the dead men there and will bring in the spare horses after they've got the supplies loaded.'

Jackson close-eyed his boss, waiting for his stormy reaction to the loss of two of his men by the man he desperately wanted to hang. Apart from the nervous chomping at the end of his cigar and the narrowing of his eyes, his boss was taking the bad news calmly, for a hair-trigger-tempered stomping man. Though it irked Ketchum no end to hear that he wasn't going to have a necktie party, yet, the killing of two of his crew didn't upset him at all, hired guns came cheap and plentiful in the Nations. He would get his hanging, he promised himself that, but he had more pressing things on his mind, the taking of the sodbusters' land.

'Do you want me to set up a big hunt for the sonuvabitch, Mr Ketchum?' Jackson said, puzzled why his boss hadn't ranted about how two so-called hard men had got themselves out-gunned by one man.

Ketchum's eyes lit up again and focused back on to Jackson. 'No,' he growled. 'Alert the sheriff at Spine Ridge that there's a killer roaming around the territory. I'll wire Judge Parker across there at Fort Smith, his marshals are supposed to uphold the law in the Nations. I haven't the time or the men to set up a big hunt. That bastard Hethridge could be heading for Texas, Kansas, wherever by now. I want the operation against the sodbusters to start rolling, Jackson. You bring the hired guns to my den in about an hour so we can discuss tactics, like which of the stinking sodbusters' barns takes fire first.'

Ketchum spat out his first cigar of the day, half-smoked and tasting like rolled horse droppings, then turned and walked back into the house.

5

Marshal Bellwood swore loudly and profanely. He re-read the Western Union flimsy the telegraph operator had handed to him as the tumbleweed wagon drew up outside Spine Ridge jail. Inside, were two prisoners waiting to be shipped back to Fort Smith, Judge Parker's jurisdiction, along with the four other prisoners the marshals' wagon held.

Judge Parker's message was brief: 'Marshal Willis to bring prisoners in. You stay in the Nations and apprehend Sam Hethridge for two counts of murder. See Spine Ridge sheriff for further details. Judge Parker, Fort Smith, Arkansas.'

Marshal Bellwood looked hard at the four prisoners in the iron-barred wagon, all killers, destined to make the one way trip to Fort Smith and give the 'Hanging' Judge the pleasure of hanging them on his fine newly built gallows that could despatch wrongdoers to hell six at a time.

Then he cast a jaundiced-eyed gaze at his deputy, Chester Willis, sitting up on the wagon seat, the reins of the two-mule team held loosely in his hands. Chester was a tall, thin, loose-limbed youth dressed in well-worn homespun jacket and pants, gear, the marshal thought, by the way it hung on Chester, must have been tailored for someone several inches shorter. His straw, part chewed brimmed hat must have graced a mule's head one time.

It was Chester's first trip into the Nations as a deputy marshal and it could well be the kid's last, Bellwood opined, if he carried out the Judge's orders. The marshal spat in the dust at his feet. Deputy Willis should still be holding the reins of a plough horse on the dirt farm he came from, not driving a tumbleweed wagon.

The two men the marshal had to pick

up from the jail were the Carr brothers, Missouri hill-billies whose robbing and killing exploits made the four prisoners in the wagon look like petty thieves. The marshal shuddered, thinking of what would happen to his greenhorn deputy on the slow haul back to Fort Smith with a wagonload of grandpappy throat-cutters squatting behind him. Somewhere along the trail the prisoners, knowing what fate lay ahead of them at Fort Smith, would think up some ploy to get the upper-hand of his gullible deputy and Judge Parker would have lost himself another marshal and missed out on having a special hanging ceremony. 'Deputy!' The marshal spat in the dirt again.

To hell with the judge's orders, Marshal Bellwoood thought angrily. He hadn't hard-assed it all the way from Fort Smith to then give his prisoners a chance to escape. He would drive the wagon back. Deputy Willis would stay here and try and pick up Sam Hethridge's trail. It would help the kid to live a little longer as a lawman. Bellwood knew of the ex-bank-robber's rep as a sneaky operator and a fast hand with both a pistol and a long gun, but the kid would be in no danger for he firmly believed Hethridge was long gone from the Nations. Naturally, he wouldn't tell Marshal Willis that, he would let the kid think he was doing a real marshal's job tracking down a double killer.

'Chester!' he called out. 'Let's get those two fellas the sheriff's holdin' chained up nice and secure in the wagon.'

* * *

Deputy Marshal Chester Willis was beaming with pride. 'Me, to track down a notorious killer on my own, Mr Bellwood?' he said. He loosened the flap on his cavalry holster and eased out the long-barrelled cap and ball Colt a fraction of an inch. He didn't want to be slow getting his gun into play when he finally confronted the killer. Suddenly his smile changed into a puzzled frown. 'What does this fella, Sam Hethridge look like, Mr Bellwood?'

'Mr' Bellwood groaned inwardly. The money Judge Parker paid his marshals only drew men who were desperate for cash, or loco like himself. Now and again a man took the badge because he believed he had a God-given mission to clear out all the bad-asses in the Nations. Which, in Marshal Bellwood's judgement, made him crazier than he was. It wouldn't take long before Marshal Chester Willis realized just how mad he was leaving a peaceful, uneventful life on a farm.

'Sheriff Kearney will give you a description of Hethridge, Deputy,' he replied. 'But only give yourself a week to try and pick up his trail. If you cut no sign by then, then you head back to Fort Smith, understand?' He smiled fatherly at Chester. 'I can't run the tumbleweed wagon regularly without a deputy backin' me up.'

Chester's moon-face grin was showing again and Marshal Bellwood climbed on to the wagon and picked up the reins. 'I'll do that, Mr Bellwood. One week from today. By then I should be bringing in a prisoner.'

Marshal Bellwood shook his head despondently. He had given the kid a chance to keep his pride and his life, and the stupid son-of-a-bitch was going to do his damnedest to get himself shot. Not by Hethridge but by one of the scores of hard men who ranged over the territory. He raised his hand to Deputy Willis, hoping to hell it wouldn't be the last time he saw the lanky hayseed who by some curse or other hankered to be one of Judge Parker's overworked, underpaid deputy marshals.

Marshal Bellwood tugged at the reins and gave a growled, 'Move ass, mules, we've a hangin' to go to!' Above the creaking and rattling of the wagon as it rocked into motion, he heard the shouted curses and dirty-mouthing of the men whose necktie party it would be.

* * *

Chester was in the Sheriff Kearney's office holding back his eagerness and impatience to start on his first hunt of a wanted man, though having the savvy to find out all he could about Hethridge. What did he look like and where he could be now? Information he could weigh up so he would get the edge on the double killer, Sam Hethridge. The advantage that should keep him alive. Mr Bellwood had trusted him with an important job, and he didn't want to let him down by making a balls-up of it by going at it wild-assed.

Hethridge's description didn't come to much. According to the sheriff, Hethridge was a medium-built man, mean-faced and more than handy with both a pistol and a long gun.

Sheriff Kearney grinned sourly. 'That

description fits almost every man in the Nations, law-abidin' and owlhooter, white and brown. Though you should have no trouble pickin' out the horse he's up on. It's a big black with a white blaze runnin' down its head.'

'Is there any hole-up in the territory he could likely be, Sheriff?' Chester asked. 'This is my first trip into the Nations and I'm kinda feelin' my way around.'

Sheriff Kearney favoured Chester with an inner pitying smile. He wanted to tell the kid to hand in his badge and go back to the farm, or wherever he came from. Maybe get a job in a general store shifting goods. Then again, he could be judging the boy too harshly. He must have been as keen and green-looking as the boy when he was young, but the goddamned war had aged him fast, forced him to develop senses he never knew he had to enable him to keep alive in that long-running hell on earth. In spite of those sympathetic thoughts, Sheriff Kearney wouldn't trust the greenhorn kid to lead him across Main Street without getting run over by a wagon. He also thought that Marshal Bellwood ought to have a bonus from Judge Parker for riding into the Nations to pick up a wagonload of genuine killing men with a pard who had yet to prove his worth.

'There is a place, Marshal Willis,' he said, 'where owlhoots lay up for a spell when the law has chased them off their stompin' grounds: Belle Starr's ranch, at Younger's Bend, forty miles west of here. Belle keeps open house for all the most wanted bad-asses from several states. Pick names off Wanted flyers, the James and the Younger boys, Blue Duck, Jim Starr and you can bet they've been holed-up at Younger's Bend. But in my opinion, Hethridge will be well clear of the Nations by now.'

The sheriff gave Chester a stern, no-nonsense stare. 'But you stay well away from Younger's Bend, do you hear, boy?' He said it as though it was almost an order. 'Your badge don't hold any sway there. You don't want to give me the upsettin' chore of seein' you decently buried. Even Judge Parker, who would send his marshals to Hell to bring back a man he wanted to string up, would balk at sendin' his lawmen to serve warrants on any hard men restin' up at Younger's Bend.'

'I'll take your advice, Sheriff. I'll move around warily,' Chester lied. He knew he wasn't a hard-bitten marshal, yet, a man who knew the next fast moves to be made to prevent himself from being gunned down by the man or men he was trailing. But he also knew he had one thing in his favour: if he didn't openly show his marshal's badge he would be, to any owlhoot he met on the trail, just what he looked like, a harmless farmboy — until he pressed the big Colt up against the surprised lawbreaker's head. Sheriff Kearney got up from behind his desk and shook Chester's hand and wished him a good hunt then led him on to the porch.

'There's a tradin' post ten miles along the Younger's Bend trail,' he said. 'You can get what supplies you need there. The skinflint who owns it will ante up the price but it will save you a ride back here, time you could use tracking down Hethridge.'

Which was as big a load of bull as he had ever spouted, the sheriff thought. The kid hadn't a cat in hell's chance of cutting Hethridge's sign. He would be raising blisters on his ass for damn all but his stubborn pride. Though it was not for him to knock the kid's end in. Time would do that for him soon enough. That was why he hadn't mentioned the coming range war to the boy. If the war did hot up, the wild men Ketchum had hired would take the marshal for one of the sodbusters they had been paid to rough up. The kid was riding into one helluva hairy situation, one he wanted no part of. It was time he set off on a fishing trip.

Chester once more thanked the sheriff for his help and advice, then swung up on to his horse, there to sit straight-backed proud as he rode out of town.

Sheriff Kearney walked back into his office to pour himself an extra large slug of whiskey and to wonder how long it would be before he was sending a wire to Judge Parker reporting the death of one of his marshals.

6

Chester dismounted outside the store and hitched his mount to the rail alongside the two horses already there. Neither animal had a white blaze running down its head, to Chester's disappointment. Then he grinned. What did he expect, bump into Hethridge on some trail or turnpike or other after only a couple of hours or so in the hunt?

He wondered if it was wise to ask the sutler, once his two customers had left, if he'd had a sighting of a rider up on a big black horse with a white head blaze. Then decided against it. His experience of sutlers, especially those who ran stores in the middle of nowhere, were that they were loose-mouthed charac-ters. The robbers' roost the sheriff of Spine Ridge had told him about, was not that far away so outlaws could

74

regularly use this trail. A dropped word from the sutler and he could be the hunted, not the hunter.

Before Chester could go into the stores to replenish his rations, the owners of the two horses stepped out. And Chester thought how right his decision not to discuss his interest in a man riding a black horse had been. The two men didn't look like ranch-hands and were definitely not farmers. They had the same stone-eyed looks as the men in the tumbleweed wagon had, men who would yank out their pistols and gun a man down with as much hesitation as they would stamp on a 'roach.

The bigger of the two men wolf-grinned. 'Why lookee here, Burl, we've found ourselves a ragged-assed sod-buster,' he said. 'Why, boy, me and my buddy here are about to pay you farmers a call. Kinda let you know Mr Ketchum's takin' over your land at what he thinks is a fair price for your pieces of dirt. Selling out is the easy way.' The big man's savage grin came back. 'We're paid to deliver the hard way if you sodbusters don't come round to acceptin' Mr Ketchum's generous offer. Ain't that so, Burl?'

'That's the way it is, Doolan,' replied Burl, his smile matching his partner's in ferocity.

Chester's nerves twanged in anger, tinged with a little fear. Rage he had to control or it could get him killed. If he tried to pull out his gun and tell them he was arresting them for threatening an officer of the law the big ugly son-of-a-bitch with the 'gator smile would shoot him dead before he had unfastened the flap of his holster. He just stood there eyeballing the pair thinking that even an expert manhunter like Mr Bellwood would reckon he was between a rock and a hard place.

The gunmen's down-putting looks suddenly stiffened Chester's resolve. Damnit! he thought, his fears burnt away by his white-hot anger. He was supposed to be a US marshal and, by thunder, it was time he acted like one. He made a grab for his pistol. Burl was quicker, his pistol barrel cracked hard against the side of his head. Chester groaned with pain and collapsed to the ground.

From the ridge, Sam saw the three men standing outside what he took to be a sutler's store. He had been scouting around the territory trying to get a feel of the land in case he had some hell-for-leather riding to do to save his hide. Then he was going to swing east to the widow Fischer's place and stand night watch over it, unbeknown to the fine-looking lady. Sam's face hardened. Mrs Fischer talked about having to be dragged from her land, but he knew she might not get the chance of putting up any sort of a fight.

The bastards, when the time came, would ride in on her Missouri brush-boy style, silently at night, holding blazing torches. The widow would not know anything was amiss until the flames were licking around her bed. If she did manage to get out of the shack unhurt, there would be nothing left for her to put up a struggle for. Sitting on watch would also give him time to work on his next move against Ketchum.

While he wanted blood for blood, Sam didn't mean the warm red blood the two ambushers had caused him to shed. Ketchum's blood was his fine house and his herd of longhorns, his power to make men jump to carry out his orders. Burning down his ranch house, scattering his cows, making him look small would be more painful to Ketchum than a gunshot wound. Sam opined it was no good thinking of a plan to do that scale of hurting. It was an operation to be carried out when the chance came and he wouldn't know that until the opportunity more or less came up and bit him in the butt.

Sam suddenly saw the glint of a pistol in one of the talkers' hands and one of them fell to the ground. 'Well I'll be durned!' he gasped. 'And here's me thinkin' they were three of Ketchum's hard men. At least one of them ain't, unless they've had a falling out.' When the man who had done the cold-cocking lifted his foot and kicked the man on the ground, Sam realized the man who was taking the punishment must be a sodbuster. And it was time he took a hand in whatever was going on down there. He couldn't stand by and let Ketchum's bully boys kick the hell out of some poor sodbuster, not when he was supposed to be on their side.

Chester's ribs were on fire and the bile rose sickeningly into the back of his throat. Blinded by tears of pain, he reached up to grab wildly for the big man's foot as it came swinging down for another bone-jarring kick. He caught it and yanked hard and had the pleasure of seeing his attacker over balance and fall backwards to the ground and grunt loudly with pain as he hit the dirt.

Burl got to his feet, dirty-mouthing. He bent down and picked up his dropped pistol. Mad-eyed, he stood over Chester. 'Sodbuster!' he spat. 'You've got yourself one painful gut-shot ticket to Boot Hill!' He thumbed back the hammer of his pistol and Chester drew himself into a tight ball in fearful anticipation of the agony he would suffer when the ball tore into his belly.

Sam's shot sent Burl howling as high pitched as a female's hysterical scream. His gun fell out of a hand mashed into a mess of blood and splintered bone. Doolan swung round, his gun half drawn. Then, just as quickly, let it slide back into its holster when he saw it was the Indian-faced Hethridge who held a gun on him, not some sodbuster.

Doolan had managed to stay alive as a hired gun by taking chances but the only chance coming his way right now was to end up with a crippled arm like poor Burl who was still howling like a kicked cur dog, or a quick death. Not wishing to risk either option by taking on Hethridge, who had all the edge, he raised his hands away from his body.

'You've got the upper hand, mister,' he said. 'For now,' he added under his breath. 'I ain't intendin' takin' you on. That busted hand of my buddy's needs seein' to pronto.'

Sam fixed the hired gun with a hard-eyed stare, pistol still aimed at him. Along with backshooting and ambushcades, honest words didn't come easy to men who hired out their guns to any cause, right or wrong, as long as it paid well. He took in the blood-drained, pain-contorted face of the man he had winged. He was well past causing him any grief, or anyone else for that matter until he learned to fire a gun with his left hand. Sam cold-smiled. And his cursing and name calling couldn't hurt him none.

'You can do that, pilgrim,' he said. 'Take your sick buddy to a croaker, then go and tell that fella who pays your due I'll be makin' a call on him some dark night, and it won't be a social visit. But you stay put till I see how the kid is.'

Chester, groaning slightly, heaved himself up on to his feet, the pistol blow and rib-kicking making him dizzy-headed and unsteady on his legs as he looked at his saviour.

'That bastard was all set to kill me, mister,' he said angrily. 'And I've no business with either of them, or seen them before! Thanks for helpin' me out, mister, I'm beholden to you.'

'Think nothing of it, boy,' replied Sam. 'It didn't seem a fair fight to me, so I thought I'd join in to kinda swing the odds in your favour so to speak.' He gave Chester a quick-eyed glance, his gun not wavering a fraction off Doolan as he did so. By his garb and the long-barrelled pistol in the cavalry holster the kid was a farmboy, not some up-and-coming gunman hoping to seek employment with Ketchum.

'Don't all you farm folk along the crick know that Ketchum of the Double Star is about to hassle you until you quit workin' your lands and he takes them over?' Sam said.

'I ain't a farmer, mister,' Chester replied. 'I'm just passin' through the territory,' hesitant to tell the man who had just saved his life he was a deputy marshal. Though his saviour seemed to side with the farmers in the trouble he mentioned, he had the same flint-eyed, poker-faced visage as the man who had been all worked up to kill him. He looked to Chester like a professional gunman, a man who would hold no good feelings towards lawmen. He didn't want to give him a good reason to push him into an early grave.

'That don't matter,' Sam said. 'It isn't safe for you to be travellin' alone when backshooters like the pair here, are on the prowl. They know their own boys, anyone else is a sodbuster. And your grandpappy's old cap-and-ball cannon you're totin' ain't goin' to be of much use to you. Why, the time it takes to draw it out of that flapped holster, haul back the hammer and pull off a shot, that's if the cap don't misfire, a man could shoot you dead and have ridden two miles away.'

Sam's voice steeled over. 'Which gets me back to you two fellas.' He waved his pistol at Doolan. 'Now you can help your buddy to mount, friend, all the cursin' and swearin' he's mouthin' ain't fit for this young boy to hear, and get his hand seen to. But before you ride out, ease out both of the rifles and drop them in the dirt.' Sam bared his teeth in a ghost of a smile. 'I ain't about to loose the edge I've got over you boys by givin' you the chance of pickin' me off with a long gun before you drop over that ridge.'

With the warning that if he ever met them on the trail again he would shoot them dead, Sam watched them ride out, holding his pistol on Doolan until he could no longer hear the wounded Burt's sobbing curses.

Chester, who had partly got over his shakes after eye-balling death real close up, did some rapid rethinking of his crazy plan to capture Hethridge. His idea of riding to Younger's Bend hoping to get the chance of throwing down on a double killer and somehow escort him all the way back to Fort Smith single-handed seemed crazier than when he first thought of it.

Chester had learned more about being a marshal in the past few minutes than he had done in the six months he had worn a badge. He would have to rein in his eagerness to prove to Mr Bellwood he was up to the job of being a marshal and stop thinking up wild plans. Play things as they came and hope the breaks came his way. The first test of his new logical reasoning could come in the next hour or so; how the hell he was going to keep himself from getting shot as a sodbuster by Ketchum's gunmen so he could stay on the hunt for Hethridge.

Sam smiled at him. 'Mr 'Drifter',' he said, 'if you ain't got any pressin' business hereabouts, I'd ass-kick it out of this section of the Nations real fast. There's nothin' but trouble ahead of you.' Sam put two fingers in his mouth and blew a piercing whistle. A few seconds later, his horse came trotting down from the ridge.

Suddenly Marshal Chester Willis was faced with a whole heap of soul searching: he was gazing at a black horse with a white blaze running down its muzzle. And he couldn't mask all the indecisive thoughts whirling around in his head.

Sam noticed the look of surprise then alarm flicker across the boy's face like some nervous tick, his close brush with death gone from his eyes. And it worried him. Why? Sam asked himself. The kid was no threat to him and he had just told him he was beholden to him for saving his life. Sam had lived a knife's edge existence most of his life, shared camps with men who'd be smiling fit to burst, just before pulling out their pistols and plugging the fella they were grinning at, dead. Though he couldn't see the kid doing that, their ways were about to part right here. In any case he hadn't the pinched-assed look of a backshooter. Close watching the kid for any further signs of why he should be feeling uneasy, he said, 'Have you made your mind up where you're headin' for, boy?'

Chester had been banking on playing things as they came in his hunt for Hethridge; events had come that fast he couldn't handle them. How could he pull a gun on a man who had just saved his life? And if he got over his clash of conscience, he would be signing his own death warrant. As Hethridge had said, he would be long dead before his big pistol cleared its holster.

'I don't rightly know where I'm bound for,' he replied. With his face starting its twitching again, still unable to think straight and not capable of lying to get himself out the dilemma he was in, he blurted out, heedless of the consequences, 'I oughta be takin' you back to Fort Smith to face charges of murder, Mr Hethridge! I'm a deputy marshal! But I reckon I can't live up to my callin'!'

Sam tried not to smile, the boy was almost in tears. He thought that 'Hanging' Judge Parker ought to be strung up himself for sending mere kids into the badlands of the Nations to do a man's job. Mock serious, he growled, 'You ain't about to throw down on me, Marshal?'

'No, I ain't,' mumbled a crestfallen Chester. 'I'm beholden to you. I was crazy to think that I had what it takes to be a marshal but I ain't that loco to think I could end up winnin' a gunfight with you, Mr Hethridge.'

'Good thinkin', boy,' Sam said. 'I ain't a posted killer, but I'll put a man down for keeps if I have to. Now we know how things stand between us, who am I supposed to have murdered?'

'According to the papers I hold on you, Mr Hethridge,' Chester said, 'The two fellas you murdered were ranch-hands.'

Sam laughed out loud. 'Ranch-hands! Why, the sonsuvbitches were two of Ketchum's hired guns, pals of the two fellas who were goin' to gut-shoot you.' Sam leaned forward, pressing his face close up to Chester's. 'See!' he snarled. 'I didn't get these cuts shavin' with a shakin' hand! They were caused by rock splash when the two fellas I *murdered* bushwhacked me!' Calming down somewhat, he added, 'If you want to find out what makes a lawman, boy, try some real law-enforcing by protectin' the sodbusters against assholes like the two I *murdered* and the two who were givin' you a hard time instead of trying to haul some innocent fella back to Fort Smith so that bastard, Judge Parker can get his kicks hangin' him.'

Chester couldn't meet Mr Hethridge's soul-penetrating gaze. He sure had made a balls-up of his first solo task as a marshal. He fervently wished Marshal Bellwood had allowed him to take the prisoners back to Fort Smith. He would have known what to do. He had no mandate as one of Judge Parker's deputies to interfere in a range war. That was the local sheriff's business, he believed. His only choice was to mount up and ride back to Fort Smith and report that he hadn't cut Hethridge's trail.

He would have done just that if it wasn't for the way Hethridge was looking at him. The horse-faced bastard was laughing at him, seeing him only as a hick of a farmboy. The rage Chester felt at being mocked cleared his confused mind and he knew exactly what he had to do. His face hardened. He may be a backwoods' boy but he didn't lack pride in himself.

He scowled angrily at Sam. 'I intend upholdin' the law here, Mr Hethridge!' he snarled. 'I intend ridin' to the Double Star wearin' my badge and arrest those hired guns who tried to kill me! And warn that rancher, Ketchum, that if his crew start harassin' the farmers, I'll take him back to Fort Smith and let Judge Parker deal with him!'

For the second time, Sam opined that the judge should swing on his own gallows for pinning a badge on a boy who should never have left his pa's farm. Though he thought the kid was growing up fast, showing true grit. Grit, Sam thought soberly, that could get him killed.

'I admire your balls, Marshal,' he said. 'But not your tactics. You've just escaped bein' shot by Ketchum's boys, why give them a second chance by ridin' bold-assed up to Ketchum's front door? Ketchum's law, not Judge Parker's law holds sway on Double Star land. You'd never ride back from visitin' that big house alive.'

Chester's face lost its defiant look. Christ, he thought, how the hell would he make it as a lawman if the only moves he could come up with were more than likely to get him killed?

Sam, seeing his doleful expression guessed that the boy's new-found grit hadn't lasted long. He began to do some thinking, fast but hard. He sighed, coming up with a decision that he could later regret. He was about to get himself a partner, an ex-hoe-toting sodbuster who harboured crazy thoughts about being a lawman. His new partner would have to measure up fast, or both of them could get dead.

'I ain't got the time for you to ponder long over what I'm about to put to you, boy,' he said. 'I've urgent business elsewhere. I'm kinda helpin' out the sodbusters, though my disagreement with Ketchum is more personal.' Sam gave one of his wolfish grins. 'So, if a righteous keeper of the law can stomach ridin' alongside a one-time jailbird and bank robber, and a man you believe murdered a coupla fellas, then you and me can be pards in the fight against Ketchum. How say you, Marshal?'

Chester didn't have to ponder long. 'Mr Hethridge,' he said, 'I ain't about to lie. This situation has got me in one helluva fix. On my own I'll be wanderin' around like a lost sheep, easy pickin's for Ketchum's hired guns. You've got yourself a pard.'

Sam gave a satisfied grunt, trying not to remember that his last partners all ended up dead. 'Get mounted, pard,' he said. 'And let's get to where I was headin' for. There could be a busy time comin' our way.'

7

Ketchum cursed. Who the hell was this son-of-a-bitch, he wondered? He was no ordinary drifter trying to earn his keep by his guns. He had killed two of his men and crippled a third. Ketchum, who had come up the hard, lawless way, had to grudgingly admit Hethridge had backbone to take on the whole Double Star. Ketchum wished the ex-bank robber had signed up with him. He was proving himself more capable with a gun than the so-called *pistoleros* he'd hired.

Jackson waited for orders from his boss after he had told him of the latest shooting. He had men ready to ride out to put the fear of God, or the Devil, in the sodbusters' hearts, unless Ketchum had changed his mind about letting the law deal with Hethridge. His boss hadn't got to be one of the biggest ranchers in the Nations by allowing any man to ring his nose. Impatient for an answer, he said, 'What do we do about Hethridge, boss?'

'Nothing, unless you meet up with the bastard,' Ketchum snapped back, waving his hands as though brushing away an annoying wasp. 'He's cocky now, having taken a couple of jabs at me and come out on top, and that will make him careless and the law will cut his sign. I want the farmers off their land before the fall. There's sheltered land along that creek where longhorns can bed down when winter sets in. That's the number-one priority, Jackson, understand?'

'Understood, boss,' replied Jackson. 'The boys are all mounted up and rarin' to go. Do they hit the widow-woman's place first?'

'I don't want to get branded in the territory as a man who drove out a poor widow from her home,' Ketchum said. He favoured his straw boss with a lopsided satanic grin. 'Seeing one of her neighbours' property going up in flames ought to persuade her to quit without any prodding from me.'

Jackson grinned back at him evilly. 'I'll tell the boys to make the flames real high so the widow can see them good.'

★   ★   ★

Kate Fischer huddled in a blanket in front of the small fire in the unlit living-room. With the coming of darkness, the wind had risen blowing a full gale along the valley and every creak and groan in the house sent her nerves jangling. Her bold words about her having to be forced off her land kicking and screaming had been nothing but blowhard words. She was too scared to go outside to get some logs to build up the fire.

Yet all her fears were not just for herself: she was worried about Mr Hethridge, how he was faring out there in the cold darkness, wounded and all. Taking on Ketchum's hired thugs was too big a task for even a hell-raiser like Mr Hethridge to tackle. Kate moaned softly. Why the hell had she ever thought she could make herself a new life in this God-forsaken land? She pulled the blanket tighter around her and tried to doze. Tomorrow's chores couldn't be put off, if she still had a farm come tomorrow.

★　★　★

An apprehensive Chester lay alongside Sam on a stretch of high ground overlooking the widow's shack. The wind was breaking up the clouds allowing the full moon to break through every now and again and light up the shack and the land around it as clear as daylight. If any raiders were coming to burn the widow out, as Mr Hethridge believed, they would be spotted long before they got within torch-throwing range. Stopping them was another matter, Chester thought soberly.

Like all Plains kids he had knocked

off tin cans from a rail fence with a .22 varmint-killing rifle but he had never fired a Winchester repeating rifle at a man before. Chester clamped his mouth tight shut. By golly, he thought, when that time came he wouldn't let his partner down, that's if he hadn't stiffened up with cold lying up on this windy ridge.

His partner hadn't been a talkative man on the ride to the shack. Apart from exchanging names and telling him he had once ridden with the Cal Butler gang, he had kept his thoughts to himself. As a young boy, Chester recollected his pa and uncles talking about the Butler gang, and rivalling them with the James and Younger boys in their heisting and robbing across the states of Missouri and Kansas. In spite of his worries and discomfort, Chester grinned to himself. Old Judge Parker across there at Fort Smith would have a heart attack if he knew that one of his marshals was a pard to a bank robber.

Sam wondered how the widow was

making out. There were no lights showing in the cabin but he hoped she hadn't gone to bed. If his ominous predictions were correct she would have to get out of the fire trap fast. He had thought about paying her a call to tell her he was standing guard over the shack, but he guessed she would have asked them both to do the guarding from the inside of a warm room. And that would lose him the slight edge he had over any attackers, the freedom to move around when the shooting started, giving the impression there were more than two of them.

Chester saw the fires first, a flickering crimson glow in the night sky. He nudged his partner in the ribs. 'There's fires away to our left, Mr Hethridge!' he gasped. 'See!'

'I see them, boy,' Sam replied, grim-voiced. 'I got it figured all wrong, the sonsuvbitches fooled me. That's the widow's neighbour's farm goin' up in flames.' He thought of the boy Jem, and the young girl, his sister, he opined, who had been on the wagon the first time he had seen him. The curses came out mule-skinner loud and profane. 'It ain't any use us squattin' up here gettin' our balls froze off,' he said, getting on to his feet. 'Not if we want to be any help to the sodbusters.'

Both of them ran to their horses and mounted up. 'We'll swing round by the front of the shack,' Sam said. 'And let the widow lady know what's happenin'.'

Kate heard shouts and jerked fully awake, face draining of blood. The fire had died out and the room was in total darkness. She picked up the shotgun and walked across to the front window and drew back the closed drapes. Her kicking and screaming time was here, though she was determined to hear one of Ketchum's bully boys scream first as he took a load of shot in his dirty hide. She sobbed her relief when, by the brilliant moonlight, she recognized Mr Hethridge. He was with another man she had never seen before. She rushed to the door, opened it and stepped out on to the porch.

'It's me, ma'am, Hethridge!' Sam called out, on catching sight of the shotgun in her hands. 'Me and my pard have been standin' guard over your place, but it looks like the bastards have hit your neighbour's holding. We're ridin' across there now. I think you'll be OK but keep a sharp lookout and if you see any flamin' torches you get to hell outa that shack, fast. Hole-up in those trees at the foot of the rise, understand? Don't be so foolish as to try and fight them off!'

Kate felt a great warmth towards Mr Hethridge. The hard man had been willing to risk his life for her. She no longer felt scared, well, not as scared as she had been, Kate admitted to herself. 'I will, Mr Hethridge,' she said. 'I promise. And you and your partner take care as well.'

'I hear you, ma'am,' replied Sam. He grinned down at her. 'Careful is my middle name.' He dug his heels into his horse's ribs. 'OK, Marshal Willis, let's do some law-enforcin'!' Chester urged his mount forward, following in his dust.

Once clear of the low ground, they both saw flames stretching across their line of sight.

'The sonsuvbitches are burnin' the fields, boy!' Sam growled. 'Ketchum intends starvin' out the sodbusters!'

Chester wasn't thinking about the burning fields, all his thoughts were focused on the men who had put the torch to them and how soon would he meet up with them. And, more importantly, would he prove himself as a peace officer to his partner when the firing began. The early excitement he was feeling was beginning to chill. Chester glanced sideways at Mr Hethridge. He didn't look worried at all about what hell they could be riding into. His partner's expressionless face seemed to have been hewed out of stone and it gave him some of his confidence back, enough, he hoped, so he could stand tall when it came to the shoot-to-kill business.

With the moon still out and a backdrop of roaring flames, Sam made out several riders driving stock towards them, men who could only be Ketchum's raiders. Like all cattlemen, Ketchum would kill sheep but not wantonly destroy horses and cattle.

'Pull over to your left, Marshal!' Sam ordered. 'We'll hit 'em on the flank, black-flag boys style, loud and fast.' Seemingly as an after thought he added, 'Can you fire that big pistol of yours on the move and hit what you've got it pointed at?'

'I don't rightly know, Mr Hethridge,' Chester replied, honestly, and embarrassedly. 'I've never had the occasion to down a fella standing still, or up on a runnin' horse.'

Sam grunted. He had known he would regret taking the kid on as his partner. It wasn't the kid's fault; he wouldn't be too happy himself admitting he was no 'Dead-eyed Dick'.

'I admire your honesty, Marshal,' he

said gruffly. 'Just get as close as you can with your shots to the fella you're aimin' at. The bang that small cannon makes oughta throw a scare into them. That's all we want to be able to do, make them break, and cut and run for it.' That's if no more regrets were about to come his way, Sam thought bleakly. 'I ain't expectin' to put them all down, boy,' he said, to try and lift his partner's spirits up somewhat. 'Remember we go in fast, shootin' and hollerin' guerilla fashion,' he continued. He gave Chester another one of his savage grins. 'We have to sow confusion in their minds, as the army top brass put it, convince them they're bein' attacked by a big bunch of men. OK?'

'OK, Mr Hethridge,' replied Chester. He would yell all right, yell loud enough to drown his fears.

Chester had heard the so-called rebel yell before, when some of Jeb Stuart's Civil War vets came riding into the settlement drunk on home-stilled whiskey, howling the Indian-like call and discharging their Dragoon Colt pistols in the air. It had frightened him as a boy, now hearing it for real, and close to, from Mr Hethridge it lifted the hairs on the back of his neck, unnerving him. He hoped it would do likewise to the men their horses were pounding down on.

Curly, in charge of the men who were driving off the farmer's stock, to be lost in the many draws and canyons in the hills, was thinking how easy the raid had gone. They had fire-balled past the front of the sodbuster's shack, peppering it with Colt shells, to keep its occupants cowering on their knees. On their way through they had seen to it that the two barns were set burning, then they moved on to their main objective, the ripening cornfields. All without any shots being fired at them.

Curly heard the blood-curdling screams. Before he could work out just who was doing the yelling and why, he saw the lance-like flames of gunshots breaking the darkness to his left, then

Doug's, the nearest rider to him, crying gasp of 'I've been hit bad!'

That left Curly and another Double Star man on their own, bringing up the drag against an unknown number of sons-of-bitches howling like a bunch of drunken Indians pulling off shots at them until the two swing men pulled back to help them to ward off the attackers. The raid had suddenly gone all sour on them. Curly yanked out his pistol, firing blindly in the direction of the nearing gun flashes.

Chester, yelling and firing as ordered, realized that Mr Hethridge had stopped yelling and was gripping his reins between his teeth and firing off two pistols. He reckoned he was seeing a one time Missouri guerilla in action. It was little wonder that the black flag, no surrender boys, raised so much hell along the Kansas–Missouri border territory during the war.

Chester, blood now running wild, rode directly at the dark shape of a rider. He saw the raider's pistol flame and felt the heat of the shell as it hissed by close to his right cheek. He gave an extra loud yell and snapped off a barely aimed shot and saw the pale, oval blob of the man's face darken suddenly then he disappeared from his sight altogether and a riderless horse sped past him.

Chester let out a blood-curdling scream any hair-lifting Indian would have been proud to echo, let alone a Johnny Reb. He had killed his first lawbreaker, a lucky head shot, but he had stood the test. Elated, he peered into the night seeking a fresh target.

The moon was still part hidden though light enough for Curly to see two saddle-horses milling around him, riderless. He had also lost sight of the badly hit Doug. Three of the boys down didn't make good odds in his and Slats's favour. Especially when one of the bastards who had jumped them was cutting loose at them with two pistols. Whoever the sonuvabitch was, he hadn't learned the killing trade walking stoop-backed behind a plough.

'Let's get the hell outa it, Slats!' he yelled. 'We've done what Ketchum wanted. Ain't no sense in gettin' ourselves killed!'

★　★　★

A cry of 'Pull up or you'll be ridin' into the stock!' from Sam, cooled Chester's blood a little. Sam drew up alongside him. 'The war's over, boy. What's left of the bastards have broke and will be asskickin' back to the Double Star to tell Ketchum the bad news.' Chester saw the gleam of his partner's teeth as he grinned at him. 'And I reckon you'll find you've emptied your gun. But you did fine, like a regular gunslinger, Marshal.'

Chester didn't hear his partner's praise, he was busy emptying the loads out of his Colt into his hand. All six were shell cases. Holy Moses! he silently gasped, how kill-crazy had he got? If another Double Star man had come at him he would have been a dead marshal. Chester's heartbeat came down to normal. He had learnt a lesson tonight, that no matter how hot the action, he had to always try and keep a cool, thinking head, if he didn't want to have it blown away.

★ ★ ★

The sun was lifting above the horizon before Sam and Chester had rounded up most of Mr Douglas's stock and were driving them back to the farm. The flames had died out but grey smoke plumes drifted across the fields and Sam could taste the acrid smell at the back of his throat. Grim-faced, he wondered what else of Mr Douglas's lifetime's work Ketchum's raiders had destroyed. The rifleman came out of the brush thirty yards ahead of them and fired. A Winchester shell passed over their heads, followed by a shout of 'Pull up your mounts and don't go for your guns, you scum!' And Sam and Chester knew it was a female, a girl, covering them with the rifle.

Emmylou Douglas tried not to shake too much as she held the rifle on the two men. Her pa had told her just to keep a lookout and to run back and warn him if she saw any Double Star riders heading back to the farm. Now here she was thinking that she could take on two hired guns when all she had shot at before were varmints.

The elder of the two definitely had the look of a gunman, the younger rider, a mere boy, hardly much older than herself, hadn't that stone-faced visage, yet, but he must have done his share of the burning of the barns and the corn. Emmylou, fierce-faced, clenched her teeth. She had made her foolish play so she had to stand by it; if they went for their pistols she would shoot the old man first then take her chance with the baby-faced boy.

'You'll be Jem's sister, missee,' Sam said, all smiles, wondering if every female he would meet up in the Nations was going to hold a gun on him. 'We're bringin' back your pa's stock. Me and my pard here, State Marshal Willis, kinda took them off the fellas who lifted them from your pa.'

A surprised Emmylou gave a relieved smile and thankfully lowered her rifle. 'You must be Mr Hethridge then,' she said. 'Jem told us about meeting you at the widow Fischer's.'

Emmylou, breathed Chester. A fine name for a fine-looking girl, he thought, gazing at her glassy-eyed like some village idiot, that the sweet-faced girl had been all set to shoot him forgotten.

Emmylou coloured up. What with wearing her pa's long hide coat for warmth, face all smoke smudged and her long red hair a shocking tangle she must look a mess and there was that young marshal ogling her as though they were at a hoe-down festival and he was about to ask her for a dance. Avoiding his gaze, she said, 'You're both welcome to come up to the house, Ketchum's men didn't burn it down, thank God. Pa will be pleased to see you, and his stock coming back in.'

In spite of how she was dressed, Emmylou couldn't ignore she was being admired by a good-looking young man. She cast her admirer a shy, sweet smile and turned and hurried along on foot to the farm to let her pa know they had welcome visitors about to call on them.

Sam did some smiling of his own on seeing the looks that passed between his young partner and the girl. The kid had come through his first gunfight OK. He still had the spirit to spark up to a pretty girl. As a man who had lived by the gun, he knew that the pair of them would need all the spirit they could muster up, and a whole heap of luck, to win out against Ketchum's hard men, but they had started well.

'Leave the stock here, pard,' Sam said. 'And let's follow that purty girl to her pa's farm. M'be I can catch up on my sleep there.' He stern-eyed Chester. 'And you as well, boy. I know you've taken a shine to that girl, but we've got dangerous times ahead of us, our nerves and reactions have to be honed real sharp. Moonin' over a female, however pleasant it is, kinda dulls a man's senses.' He smiled at Chester. 'When we've curbed in Ketchum you can do all the courtin' you want.'

8

Sam had slept long and easy, after a filling breakfast of eggs, ham and beans and fresh brewed coffee. As he ate, Sam reflected that when he did find the time to have a meal since riding into the Territory he had eaten well. First at the widow Fischer's place and now here at Mrs Douglas's table.

There had been a welcome reception of at least a dozen or so farming folk, men, women and older children. Sam reckoned that the Douglas's neighbours had showed up to help them out. And by the numbers of rifles stacked against the house porch, they were ready to fight back if the farm came under attack again. Which shouldn't have surprised him any. Most of the male sodbusters must be Civil War veterans, men who wouldn't be stomped on without retaliating.

Mr Douglas was a small but stockily-built man, looking as black as a negro field worker from fighting to put out the fires in his cornfields, who came up to Sam and Chester as they were dismounting and shook Sam's hand.

'I'm Jim Douglas,' he said. 'My daughter Emmylou has told me what you and your pard did, Mr Hethridge. We farmers are beholden to you both. And accordin' to Jem your grievance with Ketchum is personal, Mr Hethridge, but whatever it is it's still helpin' out us farmers.'

'No offence to you, Marshal Willis,' Mr Douglas said, on being told by Sam that Chester was a US marshal. 'And I thank you for what you've already done for us, but it will take a troop of horse soldiers to put Ketchum in his place.'

'I ain't been sent here by Judge Parker to settle a range war,' replied Chester. He gave a flicker of a smile after glancing at Sam. 'I'm in the Nations to try and rope in a dangerous killer. I kinda got forced into this dispute so I reckon I ought to stay until it's cleared up.' He smiled confidently at Mr Douglas. 'At least it's another gun against Ketchum.' Then he looked around hoping to catch sight of Miss Emmylou Douglas.

'Is that coffee I can smell, Mr Douglas?' Sam asked. 'I don't know what I crave more, a good sleep, or a cup of coffee.'

Jim Douglas smiled. 'All the folk here have the same craving, Mr Hethridge. It's been one helluva night for us all. Ma and a few of the womenfolk are fixin' breakfast. I'm expecting a wagon-load of men from the other holdings along the creek to come in soon. They'll stand guard while the rest of us can eat and catch up on our sleep. You and your pard are welcome to share what the women are dishing up.' The farmer's face hardened. 'It don't make tactical sense to wear ourselves out on the first raid; there'll be many such nights to come before I can rebuild my barns.'

Chester was also tired and hungry

but his tiredness vanished when he saw it was Emmylou who was pouring out the coffee.

*   *   *

Sam got up from the table and thanked Mrs Douglas for the food. 'I'll sneak a coupla hours sleep in the barn of yours that's still standin', Mr Douglas,' he said. 'But if Ketchum's wild boys show up again you holler out.'

Jim Douglas pointed out of the window. He grinned. 'Your pard doesn't seem to mind losing out on a few hours' shuteye, Sam. Him and Emmylou look as though they've hit it off.'

Sam looked out on to the porch and saw Chester and Emmylou sitting side by side, talking.

'The kid needs a few pleasurable moments, Jim,' Sam said. 'Last night was his first taste of the killin' business and as you rightly stated it mightn't be his last trip down that bloody road. Though he totes a marshal's badge the

117

kid ain't anything but a Missouri farmboy, but he's learnin' a peace-officer's way fast.' He smiled at Mr Douglas. 'I'll go out the back way to the barn; I was young myself once, I think.'

'I heard you tell Pa that you're tracking down a notorious killer, Chester,' Emmylou said.

'That's what Judge Parker across there at Fort Smith is payin' me to do, Miss Emmylou,' Chester replied, in what he hoped was a genuine bold-assed peace-officer voice.

Real bold-assed, Emmylou inched closer to Chester until she could feel his warmth through the thin fabric of her dress. Looking him directly in the eyes, she said, softly, 'Will you come by this way after you rope in that killer, Chester?'

Emmylou had looked pretty when he had first seen her, Chester thought; now, all cleaned up and wearing a dress and feeling her soft warmness, her prettiness was catching at his breath. 'As sure as hell I'm coming back!' he wanted to blurt out, but his manly pride not wanting Emmylou to know she had him well and truly hooked, he said, still in his marshal's no-nonsense voice, 'It depends on what section of the Nations Judge Parker sends me to. But if I can I'll swing by this way again, I promise.' Chester had already made up his mind that even if the judge sent him as far north as the Kansas border he would, come hell or blizzards, pay another call on Miss Emmylou Douglas.

Emmylou smiled. 'I'll hold you to that, Marshal Willis,' she said, getting on to her feet. 'Now, you must get some sleep, like Mr Hethridge, while you can.' Her face clouded over. 'From now on it will be Mr Ketchum who decides whether we sleep or not.'

Reluctantly, Chester agreed it was time he rested up. He owed it to Mr Hethridge to be wide awake, alert to any danger coming their way when they rode out to take the war to Ketchum. Whatever plan his partner came up with, it would entail shooting. And with sudden, cold logic Chester realized that apart from Judge Parker sending him to the far corners of the Nations there were other reasons why he might not see Emmylou again: he could get himself killed by one of Ketchum's hired guns.

'I'll see you before we ride out, Emmylou,' he said, and turned and walked over to the barn, not feeling bold-assed at all now.

9

Ketchum bared his teeth in a silent wolf-like snarl. So he had a fight on his hands, he thought angrily. Damnit, he'd give those bastard sodbusters a war all right. Curly had told him how the raid hadn't worked as planned and how three of his crew had been killed. 'Who was doing the shooting?' he asked. 'The sodbusters?'

'There's no tellin' who they were, or how many of them, boss,' lied Curly. 'Bein' they came at us outa the dark. But one of them was a real sharpshootin' bastard, cuttin' loose at us with two pistols, harin' in on us at a gallop.'

Ketchum knew who the two-gun shootist was. Hethridge had showed his deadly hand again. The bank robber must have been hired by the sodbusters and he was proving his worth. It had been a mistake on his part not realizing how big a danger Hethridge could be. He had to be dealt with, or the sodbusters would take heart and could bring the war to the Double Star. Ketchum did some hard thinking. Then, slowly, a smile as cruel as his snarl crept over his face. He would give the sodbusters a real shooting war, hammer them until they would be glad to quit their lands.

But it was a killing business the Double Star couldn't be seen to be linked with, or Judge Parker would have no hesitation in sending in the army against him, and he could kiss goodbye to his grand ambitions to be the top dog in the territory.

The men he would need to hire would have no connection with the ranch. They would be strangers in the territory, men with prices on their heads, dead or alive. Suchlike owlhoots were always drifting into the Nations to hole-up for a spell. And the place to find them was the robbers' roost at Younger's Bend, Belle Starr's place.

'Get my horse saddled up, Jackson!' he called out. 'We're going to see who's paying a call on Belle Starr.'

★ ★ ★

Four men were sitting on Belle Starr's front porch when Ketchum and his straw boss rode in. Hard men, men who killed with an easy conscience to get their wherewithal, were regular visitors to Younger's Bend, but Jackson opined he was eyeballing some of the meanest-looking men ever to grace Belle Starr's porch. His hand moved closer to his pistol butt.

He heard the man, who was whittling at a stick with a knife big enough to cut a man's head off, say loud enough for him and Ketchum to hear, 'Hey, Phil, do you reckon these two fellas are a coupla of the Hangin' Judge's marshals come to serve warrants on us?'

Phil! The realization who the ugly-faced bastards were hit Jackson like a blow from a fist. His hand moved clear of his pistol as though his fingers had been burnt, not wanting to have that big knife sticking out of his chest.

'Those fellas are the Craddock gang, Mr Ketchum,' he whispered, side-mouthed. 'That fella with the knife must be Josh, Phil Craddock's loco brother.'

Ketchum grunted. The Craddock gang's killing and robbing trail led all across Kansas and Missouri, not fearing to face anyone, man or devil. He couldn't choose a better bunch of men for the task he wanted them for. He rode right up to the four men. His icy gaze swept over them. Ketchum hadn't got where he was by being intimidated by looks or threats. 'I know who you are,' he said. 'So it's only polite you should know who I am. I'm Silas Ketchum, I run the Double Star spread, a piece south of here, and I reckon I can speak plainly to you gents.'

Phil Craddock, a lantern-jawed, unshaven individual grinned at his brother then looked up at Ketchum, his eyes holding none of his smile. 'That's the only language we country boys know, Mr Ketchum. We're all ears.'

'I'm having a little trouble with some sodbusters, Mr Craddock,' Ketchum said. 'Over the disputed rights of some land. I was hoping that you and your boys, unless you have pressing business elsewhere, would be willing to persuade the sodbusters to see things my way. I'm not fussy how you do the persuading and you can name your own price.'

Josh stopped his whittling and got to his feet. 'What do you think, Phil?' he said.

Phil's smile almost showed warmth this time. 'Well, seein' that Mr Ketchum has put forward a genuine proposal we can't rightly turn it down without discussin' it. You step down, Mr Ketchum, and tell us more about the trouble you spoke of. I reckon, being all of us are plain-speakin' gents, we oughta be able to agree to a price that will make me and my boys happy without too much arguin'.'

★ ★ ★

Ketchum and Jackson rode back to the Double Star, the rancher feeling good knowing that he would soon own all the grass right up to the creek. Being a good judge of men he had no doubts that the Craddock brothers would fulfil their part of the deal.

'You can put the boys on regular ranch work, Jackson,' he said. 'Keep them well clear of the sodbusters' lands. The war is about to get bloody and we don't want to be seen to be mixed up in it in any way.'

A troubled Jackson gave a curt nod of understanding. Burning out sodbusters and sheep men were one thing, letting loose a bunch of gun-crazy killers on the sodbusters and their families choked at his craw — though the straw boss kept his uneasy thoughts to himself.

10

All the folks still at the Douglas farm watched a refreshed, well-fed Sam and Chester mount up and ride out, and wished the pair of them all the luck in the world.

'While you were sleeping, old-timer,' a grinning Jim Douglas said, 'We brought the stock in and buried the three fellas you and Chester put down.'

Jim would have liked to have them to stay on the farm to boost up his defences in case of another attack by Ketchum's raiders, but what Hethridge had said about it being safer for the sodbusters for him to stay well clear of the farms was sound advice. Jim reckoned that by now Ketchum would have figured out who had killed his boys and would have set up a big hunt for Hethridge. If he even got so much as a hint that Sam had been on his farm, the rancher would hit him with all the men he had, burn down everything that would burn.

'You take care out there, boys,' he said soberly. And don't forget on every fourth day, Jem, or Emmylou, will drop you some supplies at the foot of the west face of Indian Butte. You can't miss it, it's a big lump of rock standing on its own an hour's ride along the trail from here.'

'You don't send your youngsters out unless it's safe to do so, Jim,' Sam said, hard-eying the farmer. 'Me and the boy can tighten up belts for a few extra days.'

'They'll be OK,' replied Jim. 'There's no farms within six miles of the butte, Ketchum's boys have no need to be in that section of the territory.'

His partner was right, Chester thought. He would rather chew on his saddle than put Emmylou in danger. She was standing there on the porch alongside her ma, trying not to cry at him having to leave her, or so he wanted to believe.

'OK, Marshal,' he heard Mr Hethridge say. 'It's time we let these Christian folk get on with putting things right here and see if we can find any more of Ketchum's hired guns to cut loose at with Colt shells.'

Chester was about to wave, casually to Emmylou, though still retaining his poker-faced US marshal's look. Mr Hethridge's matter-of-fact words of how they were going to hunt down two-legged wolves somehow slackened his facial muscles and stayed his hand, and made him put all thoughts, however pleasurable, from his mind. Once again he had to concentrate on how he would dodge the hot lead the Double Star men could soon be sending at him.

A disappointed Emmylou, expecting at least a smile from Chester, wondered if he had forgotten her already! And like some saloon hussy she had pressed herself against him when they were sitting on the porch. Would have allowed him to have kissed her if he had plucked up enough courage to do so. Damn it, she thought, she was acting selfishly, Chester and Mr Hethridge were risking their lives for the farmers. Eyes damp, Emmylou made up her mind that the next time she saw Chester she would put her arms around him and kiss him, even if every family along the creek were watching. Emmylou suddenly felt a warm glow, a tingly sensation, all over her body. She gave a secretive smile. Now she was beginning to feel like a flighty hussy.

'What's your plan, Mr Hethridge?' Chester said, when they were well clear of the farm.

Sam gave him one of his cold-eyed smiles. 'I ain't committin' myself to makin' any plans, boy,' he replied. 'I did that once, made a plan, a plan to rob a bank. And my goddamned plan got all my pards killed and me, bein' the lucky one, ten years in the State Pen. I don't favour makin' any more plans. What we do is to watch what goes on at the Double Star and try and make a balls-up of any plan Ketchum dreams up to harass the sodbusters.'

★　★　★

It was the second day they had kept the Double Star ranch under surveillance and had seen no signs of activity other than the usual movement of the hands carrying out regular ranch chores.

They had, since leaving the creek, ridden across the low ground, watching out for any tell-tale trail dust of riders until they had reached a well-timbered ridge overlooking the Double Star's big house without being spotted by any of the crew or hired guns. Dismounting below the ridge line, they drew out their long guns and walked the few steps to the razor-back crest.

'Here is as good a place as any,' Sam said, pointing with his rifle at a rocky ledge running along the ridge for several feet. He grinned. 'It ain't exactly feather-bed soft, but it's better than lying down on damp grass being my spell in the Pen left me with a touch of the screws in most of my joints. And we could be here till nightfall; Ketchum won't send his boys out raidin' in the daytime.'

They took turns to stand the night watches. Whoever wasn't on duty would brew the coffee, warm some beans for the two of them over a low burning fire set back in a small cave on the reverse slope of the ridge, before wrapping themselves in their blankets to try and snatch a couple of hours' fitful sleep.

By nightfall, with still no signs of any raiding parties leaving the ranch, worry and uncertainty was gnawing away at Sam's insides. Why the hell was Ketchum holding back his attacks on the sodbusters? Had the killing of his men drawn in his horns, realizing that the price he was paying for the grass he wanted was too high? One thing was for sure, he and the boy couldn't stay up on this ridge much longer. His partner's face was as pale and strained as his must be.

As they were having their meal, Sam spoke of his worries to Chester.

'Something ain't right about Ketchum sittin' tight on his ass down there, Marshal,' he said. 'What I saw of him the sonuvabitch didn't have the cut of a man who quits easy on something he has set his mind on. So, instead of turnin' in, I intend to do a little scoutin' around, just in case any of his boys have sneaked by us.'

'Between us, Mr Hethridge,' Chester said, 'we ain't had our eyes, or ears, off that ranch since we climbed up on this ridge.'

'M'be so, m'be so, boy,' replied Sam. 'But I've got a gut-feelin' that Ketchum has set some big trouble for the sodbusters in motion and what that is could be just about to happen.' He smiled. 'Of course, it could only be those goddamned warmed-up beans playin' hell with my guts. But it don't do no harm to check things out. I'll follow the main trail off the ranch so if you see any activity down there don't tackle it on your own, understand? You ass-kick it along the trail and catch me up. Then we can decide what should be done. OK?'

'OK,' replied Chester. His guts were also playing him up, thinking of the trouble Mr Hethridge felt was about to occur could hit the Douglas farm again.

* * *

The Caxton shack was all in darkness when the Craddock gang closed in on it, which suited Phil Craddock's purpose. Being woken up in the middle of a deep sleep to find your home going up in flames about your ears tended to throw a man off balance more than somewhat. It only gave him a few seconds to choose whether he should save his family, or take on the men who were torching your shack. And Phil knew from experience most men would try and save his kin first.

'Bert,' Phil said. 'Burn down the barn. Chuck, scatter the stock. Kill anyone who comes at you with a gun.' He bared his teeth in a humourless grin. 'Me and Josh will raise hell at the shack.'

Calvin Caxton, lying in bed alongside his wife, woke with a start on hearing the sound of breaking glass in the living-room. He rolled out of bed, grabbing the shotgun resting up against the wall close by him as he got on to his feet. He padded across the room to the door, opened it and saw the coal-oil-soaked rag torch in the middle of the living-room, its flames already spreading fiery channels across the rug and licking at the walls and drapes.

For a few seconds he stood there, horror-struck, mouthing words he had never used in front of his wife before. 'Meg!' he then shouted. 'Wake up! The place is burning! Get the kids out by the back door, hurry!'

Calvin heard the frightened cries of his two young boys as their mother bundled them out of the house. All that could be saved had been saved. Now it was time he fought back by putting two barrels of shot-gun lead in the dirty hide of the first fire-raising son-of-a-bitch he got a sighting on.

Calvin, shielding his face with his arm, edged his way around the flames. He made it to the door, coughing and eyes stinging and watering. He opened it and stepped out on to the porch. Silhouetted against a fiery backcloth he was an easy target for Phil Craddock. The two shots from his pistol hurled Calvin back into the room, mercifully a dead man before he fell into the flames.

Sam saw the ominous glow like an early sunrise in the far sky. He cursed. Sitting up there on the ridge had been a complete waste of time; another poor sodbuster and his family was feeling Ketchum's heavy hand. But how the hell had the raiders slipped by him and the boy? he asked himself angrily. As his young pard had said, they hadn't taken their eyes off the ranch. Yet he could see the proof that someone's farm was under attack. He pulled his horse's head round and rode back to the ridge, and his partner, still worrying about how they had slipped up by keeping a careless watch.

Chester rolled over on to his side as he heard a slight rustling behind him. 'It's me!' he heard Mr Hethridge say. He gave a weak grin and lowered his rifle. 'You came up on me as quiet as it has been down there since you left, Mr Hethridge.'

'It ain't as quiet back along that creek, pard,' Sam said, hard-voiced. 'Another sodbuster's home is goin' up in flames.'

'Is it the Douglas's place again?' Chester asked hoarsely, sick in the stomach about what Emmylou could be suffering.

'I don't think so, the fire's north of the Douglas's farm. Though wherever it is we'll be too damn late to be of any help.' replied Sam.

They risked their own necks as well

as their horses on the fast ride to the blazing farm, Chester asking no more questions about how Ketchum's men had sneaked off the ranch without being spotted. By the look on Mr Hethridge's face, his partner wasn't in a talking mood. Chester guessed that Mr Hethridge was blaming himself for the blaze for allowing Ketchum to fool him.

A single shot, a warning one, Sam hoped, was fired at them as the trail dipped down into the creek valley several hundred yards away from the burning building.

'It's me, Sam Hethridge and Marshal Willis!' he yelled out, before nervous trigger-fingers cut loose a hail of lead at them. 'Pull up, boy!' he called out. 'And let them see us.' He drew his mount up in a sliding back leg dust raising halt. Chester, slightly slower in his reactions, pulled up his horse ahead of Sam.

Two men, holding rifles stepped up to them. 'We're sorry about the shot, Mr Hethridge,' one of the farmers said.

'But we're kinda edgy. It's been a bad business along at the Caxtons' place, the murderin' sonsuvbitches have killed Calvin.'

Chester saw Mr Hethridge's face get longer and meaner-looking as they rode along the creek to what was left of the Caxtons' home. Several more armed farmers were standing around the fire-gutted building. There was still enough light from the dying down blaze for Sam to recognize that one of them was Jim Douglas. He stopped alongside him.

'Bad business here, Sam,' a grim-faced Douglas said.

'So I've heard,' replied Sam. 'The bastards caught us nappin'.'

'The flames had too big a hold for us to do anything but watch the place burn,' Jim Douglas said. 'Calvin, the poor bastard, is still inside. Ma has taken his wife and his two boys back to our place. It ain't fitting for her to see what's left of her man when the place gets cool enough for us to go in and get

Calvin out. We'll give his bones a Christian burial, then a bunch of us are going to ride to the Double Star and burn down Ketcham's fine house and shoot dead any sonuvabitch who gets in our way.'

'Ketchum's hired guns didn't do this, Jim,' Sam said. 'Me and the boy here, have been watchin' the ranch like a coupla hawks for two days and I'll stake my life that no rider left that ranch other than to do ranch chores. If you farmers attack the Double Star you'll play right into the bastard's hands. He'll sicc the law on to you. Then those of you who ain't been shot dead will be in jail. While you're inside Ketchum will take your land; your womenfolk won't be able to stop him.'

'You ain't asking us to believe that Ketchum had no hand in this?' Douglas waved a hand at the smoke-smouldering ruins. 'Are you, Mr Hethridge?'

'No, I ain't,' replied Sam. 'All I'm sayin' is that the gun-hands Ketchum has workin' as ranch-hands didn't do it. Ketchum must have hired some more guns workin' independent of the Double Star crew, killin' men. It looks as though Ketchum has lost patience with you mule-stubborn sodbusters and is prepared to fight real dirty and still come up smelling like roses.'

'What the hell are we farmers supposed to do, Sam!' Jim Douglas retorted angrily. 'Sit in our homes waiting to be burned out?'

'No,' replied Sam. 'We find out who the bastards are who did this. How many there are of them. And, importantly, where they hole-up between raids. Then deal with the bastards,' Sam added grimly.

'I think I know where, Mr Hethridge,' Chester said. 'The sheriff at Spine Ridge told me of a place called Younger's Bend run by a Mrs Belle Starr. He said that wanted men as far afield as Kansas and Missouri hole-up there one time or another.' Chester didn't tell his partner he intended going to see if Sam was using Younger's Bend as a hideout.

'Yeah, Chester's right,' said Jim Douglas. 'We've heard Belle Starr's place is a home-from-home for owl-hoots, but we've never had any trouble from Belle's visitors before.'

'M'be because no one's paid them to cause you sodbusters trouble before,' Sam said. 'Come daylight we'll . . . no, it better be just me, Marshal Willis. No offence but you ain't got the mean-eyed look of a lawbreaker. And the hard men whose handiwork you can see before you are natural born suspicious men. Me, bein' the genuine article, oughta be welcomed with open arms at Younger's Bend. We ain't got the time to make up an owlhoot's existence for you, Marshal, that will stand up to any nosy questioning.'

Sam grinned on seeing Chester's disappointed-looking face. 'That don't mean you ain't ridin' with me; we're pards, ain't we?' he said. 'You can lie low someplace, within long-gun range of Belle Starr's shack, or whatever, as my ace in the hole if things go wrong for me. As I've already told you, it don't do to take unnecessary risks.'

11

Sam had forded the Canadian at one of its loops and was riding up the sandy, sloping bank to the stoutly built shack set well above the flood-line of the river. He had left Chester on the far bank out of sight of anyone in the shack, covering his approach to the so-called 'thieves' kitchen', or to give him back-up fire if he had to rib-kick it back across the river. Or so he had led Chester to believe, not wanting the boy to lose his new-found confidence by thinking that his partner didn't fully trust him yet.

Sam wasn't expecting any trouble at Younger's Bend. His credentials as an outlaw ranked alongside any other bank robber in the Mid-West. And if what he had been told about Belle Starr's hospitality towards lawbreakers was true, as a one-time member of the Cal Butler gang she would welcome him with open arms.

By cutting sign at the burnt-out farm they knew they were hunting four men. In which direction they had ridden off they hadn't been able to tell, their tracks petering out once the raiders had reached hard ground.

Sam noticed the tracks of several horses leading up to the shack; whether some of them were made by the men they were hunting he couldn't tell. And he could only see two horses in the corral at the side of the shack. So, it didn't seem he was going to have the luck of throwing down on the four while sitting down having tea with gunbelts slung over the backs of their chairs.

He reckoned that more subtle tactics would have to be used if he wanted to bring the killers to book, such as speaking forked-tongued, like the Indians thought all white-eyes spoke, to Mrs Belle Starr. If he could fool her, she could maybe point him in the direction of the raiders. That is if they had been staying at Younger's Bend and were still in the territory. He was relying on a lot of 'ifs' coming right for him, Sam opined sourly.

The woman who stepped out on to the porch as he came up to the shack had Sam letting out his breath in a low surprised whistle. She was dressed in a long red velvet gown that scuffed up the dust on the porch boards as she walked. In her fine gown she reminded Sam of the whore he'd paid good money to have in a high-class cat house in Kansas City, in the days when the gang was on a roll.

Then the resemblance of a welcoming, smiling, short-time girl faded when he got close enough to see the gimlet-eyed hatchet face, that made the heavy pistol in the well-filled shellbelt across her slim waist something more than a dress decoration. Sam opined he wouldn't step down from his horse until Mrs Belle Starr invited him to do so. He wouldn't want it to be put about that he had been shot off his horse by a female.

He touched the brim of his hat in a curt greeting and favoured her with a smile. 'I'm Sam Hethridge,' he said. 'I once rode with the Cal Butler gang way up in Kansas and Missouri.' His smile broadened. 'We were kinda in the bankin' business, transferrin' cash from the banks safes into our pockets with the points of our pistols. Now all the boys are dead, exceptin' me.'

'I've heard of the Cal Butler gang,' Belle Starr said. 'I hail from Missouri myself. But you haven't rode all the way to Younger's Bend, Mr Hethridge, just to tell me the story of your misfortunes,' she added gruffly, though her face had no longer the sharp lines of a hard-assed *pistolero*.

'No I ain't, Mrs Starr,' replied Sam. 'I thought that m'be you could help me out. While I was doin' my ten years in Kansas State Pen, I came up with the idea of raisin' my own gang when I'd done my time.' Now, seeing he had a sympathetic ear, Sam's lies came out easy. 'Take up my old trade of bank robbin' again. But with bein' out of circulation for so long, all the reliable fellas I knew are either dead or rottin' inside some Pen or other. And I ain't riskin' been thrown back into jail for the rest of my natural by ridin' with a bunch of greenhorn kids who fancy themselves as bona-fide hold-up men. I was told while I was inside that the likeliest place to find any old gunhands was here at Younger's Bend.' Sam glanced about him. 'Though right now that don't look so.'

'Mr Hethridge,' Belle Starr said. 'If you had called on me a couple of days earlier you m'be could have raised a gang. The Craddock brothers and two of their buddies were here.' Belle paused for a moment. 'Though to be truthful, I couldn't see Phil Craddock taking orders from who he would think was an old has-been — no offence intended, Mr Hethridge — but I'm just telling you the way Phil would view it. No one but him has to be top dog.'

Sam shrugged. 'That's just my goddamned luck, Mrs Starr,' he said, as though he was disappointed. He probed a little further. 'I take it they've left the Nations then?'

Belle Starr shook her head. 'I don't think so,' she replied. 'I was in town when they left, but the hand who looks after my stock told me the boys rode off not long after two riders came up to the house and had words with Phil. One of the men was Silas Ketchum who runs the Double Star, the biggest spread hereabouts.' Belle smiled. 'Your guess is as good as mine for what business Ketchum needs four hard guns for. I'm sure it isn't for branding his mavericks.'

Sam gave an inner smile of satisfaction. His partner's tip had paid off. From this robbers' roost they ought to have a fair chance of picking up the raiders' trail again. And an added bonus was now they knew the names of the sons-of-bitches.

'Of course you're welcome to stay here, Mr Hethridge,' Sam heard Belle

Starr say. 'The Craddocks could swing by this way once they've done what Ketchum's paid them to do. Though, as I said, Phil will need a lot of persuading, or a bigger cut of the pot, for him to take orders from you.'

'Thanks for the kind offer, Mrs Starr,' replied Sam. 'But I kinda like bein' on the move. Ten years stuck between four walls gives a man a hankerin' for the wide-open spaces, come hail or snow. I'll drift south, Texas m'be.' He grinned at Belle. 'I've heard that hard men come by the barrelful in the Lone Star State. If I meet up with Mr Craddock on the trail I'll put my proposal to him and see if he favours it.'

A thoughtful Belle Starr watched her caller splash his way across the Canadian. She shook her head slowly. The old guns were on the way out. The Youngers, especially Cole, and the James boys, had a sense of honour and loyalty in their make-up. The new breed of outlaws, like the Craddock brothers, scared her. They were murderous assholes who wouldn't even honour their parents.

Chester joined up with Sam as soon as he knew neither of them could be seen from the shack.

'Did you strike lucky, Mr Hethridge?' he asked excitedly.

'That I did, boy, that I did. The four raiders were stayin' with Belle Starr until a coupla days ago, then that stompin' man, Mr Ketchum, came along and hired them. We're lookin' for the Craddock brothers and the two other bastards who ride with them, Marshal.' Sam gestured over his shoulder with his thumb. 'They're somewhere out there plannin' their next raid and it's up to us to come up with a scheme of our own, but fast, to stop any more killin's.'

12

Prairie Dog town wasn't really a town but a scattering of lopsided, sunbleached shacks erected by buffalo hunters, thirty or so years before on a real prairie dog town. With the big shaggies long since almost shot out of existence, the hunters had left to take up other trades, leaving their 'town' to the outlaws and the aimless drifters wanting a little more comfort than camps on the open plains.

The Craddock gang were sitting in the biggest shack, which did service as a sutler's store and a saloon. In a blanketed-off corner, a man, not too particular about the facial beauty of a woman, could, for a small price, satisfy his urges with the only whore in town.

'Ain't we gonna start earnin' the other half of our due, Phil?' Charlie Casper said. 'I can think of better places to spend my cut than here in this rat hole, drinkin' rotgut liquor even an Injun would turn his nose up at. And how the hell Josh can pay out good cash for beddin' that horse-faced woman has me beat.'

Phil grinned. 'Josh is kinda hot-blooded, Charlie. But waitin for him to cool down somewhat ain't the reason we're stayin' in this apology of a town. On our first raid that sodbuster wasn't expectin' trouble. By now all the sodbusters will be sittin' by their windows in their nightshirts holdin' rifles and shotguns makin' sure they'll not be surprised again. Give them a few peaceful nights then they'll get tired of standin' watch. And that's when we'll show up.'

Josh's yell of 'You thievin' bitch!' then a woman's high-pitched scream of pain had the three of them jerking upright in their chairs.

Josh, yanking aside the blanket came into view. Face working in anger he snarled 'The little whore tried to take my roll from my pants pocket while I was gettin' my shirt back on!' He grinned savagely. 'I prettied up her face with my knife. It'll be a while before she gets herself another customer.'

'Boys,' the sutler said, stopping his stocktaking. 'You look old enough to know your own business, but my advice is to get the hell outa Prairie Dog, pronto. That girl your buddy there carved up some, will by now be tellin' her pa and her four brothers who used the knife on her. Her kin's part Apache, bad Apache and they'll quick-foot it over here and lift your hair as slick as any full-blood Injun.' He shot Josh a baleful glare. 'And they'll be mad-assed enough to burn down this place with me in it. You gents have been here long enough to note that there ain't no law here in Prairie Dog.'

Phil favoured his brother with a scowling look. 'If you had the savvy to have kept your pants on, we wouldn't have to squat out there in the cold someplace till we're good and ready to hit the sodbusters again.'

Charlie's look at Josh was as unfriendly as Phil's had been. 'When do we start the fireworks, Phil?' he said. 'I reckon we should go fire-ballin' along that crick and raise as much hell as we can at every sodbuster's shack we hit. Then ride up to the Double Star and get the rest of our due from Ketchum, then go south. It don't make sense stayin' in the Nations longer than we have to watchin' our back trail because Josh there has raised up a blood feud agin us. I'm kinda partial wantin' to hang on to my hair. What say you, Bert?'

'I can't disagree with your reason, Chuck,' Bert replied. 'Though I ain't got any hair to lose I'd like to be alive and enjoy spendin' my share.'

For once Phil acted on an opinion other than his own. Even if Charlie hadn't been right, if he went against Charlie and Bert he would lose half his gang, and the rest of the payment Ketchum had promised him when the sodbusters began moving off their land. Silently cursing Josh, he swallowed his pride. 'OK, boys,' he said. 'Let's mount up and do as Charlie says. We're not bein' paid to fight an Injun war.'

*   *   *

Jackson and two ranch hands, rounding-up and branding mavericks on the very edge of the Double Star range, saw four riders heading south-east, and fast. The straw boss guessed that they were his boss's latest hirings getting set up to give some poor sodbuster an early grave. He had heard about the killing of Caxton and the destruction of his home while picking up stores in Spine Ridge and it hadn't gone down well with him. The killing had been put down as the work of a band of renegade whites passing through the territory on their way to Texas. Ketchum, as he had said, was in the clear. He shrugged. It was none of his business. He was paid to look after the longhorns. He picked up the branding-iron.

★   ★   ★

'Have you come up with a plan, Mr Hethridge?' Chester asked. He didn't know how skilled his partner was, but even if he had Indian blood in him it would be a formidable task to pick up tracks of four riders on ground as hard as bedrock. Attempting to pick up their tracks on the several main trails that cut across the territory would be a waste of time; there would be dozens of hoof prints in the dirt; which ones would they follow?

And worrying away at Chester's inside was the knowing fear that the longer it took to hunt down the Craddock gang the greater danger Emmylou and the rest of the farming families would be living under.

'No, Marshal, I ain't,' repeated Sam. 'Other than we head towards the nearest farm on the wild chance that the Craddock gang must have come this way and they'll hit the first place they come to.'

As worried as he was about Emmylou's well-being Chester couldn't come up with a better suggestion.

'Hold it, boy!' Sam said, suddenly, and pulled up his horse. 'Can you smell it?'

Chester drew up his own mount and drew in a deep breath, and caught a slight tangy smell in the air.

'That's a brandin' camp-fire,' Sam said. 'You can smell the scorched hide.' He scowled. 'And the ranch-hands at that fire more than likely will be Double Star men, fellas we don't want to pass the time of day with.'

'It's too late, Mr Hethridge,' an alarmed Chester said, pointing over his partner's shoulder. 'One of the bastards is coming our way!'

Sam twisted round in his saddle and saw the Double Star straw boss driving a calf in front of him coming out of a dip in the ground. He cursed softly.

'That's Ketchum's right-hand man. Get set to rib-kick it back the way we come because if I have to plug him, the ranch-hands at that fire will hear it and come boilin' over yon ridge howlin' for our blood.'

Jackson saw them and came to a quick decision. Holding his hands well away from his body he called out 'I ain't drawin' a gun on you, Hethridge, I want to parley!'

Sam gave Chester a puzzled, what-the-hell look before shouting 'You can come on in, mister! I'm all ears!' Though his hand rested on his pistol butt. The last time he had been caught out it had cost him ten years of his life. Dropping his guard again could end it, and his young partner's as well.

'I ain't got much time, Hethridge,' Jackson said. 'If one of my men at the camp sees me talking to you, Ketchum will string me up.'

'You get up on to that ridge, boy,' Sam ordered. 'You oughta see their camp from there. If any of the fellas come this way scoot back down here and we'll make ourselves scarce and save 'Mr Straw Boss' from a rope necktie. OK?'

'OK, Mr Hethridge,' Chester said, and kneed his horse up the gradual rise to the rim-line.

'Now we'll parley, friend,' Sam said curtly.

'I reckon you've figured out that Ketchum has hired a new bunch of gun hands,' Jackson said.

'Yeah, I know,' replied Sam. 'I saw some of their bloody handiwork. And I know who the sonsuvbitches are, the Craddock gang. What I want to know is where they are now and what devilry they're thinkin' up to inflict on the sodbusters, and how soon.'

'A little over an hour ago,' Jackson began, 'I saw the four of them ridin' south-east, towards the German widow's farm. I figure she'll be safe till dark, then it'll be up to you and your pard to do what you think you oughta do. The way you put down those hired guns must mean that you're workin' for the sodbusters.'

Sam looked Jackson directly in the eyes, the straw boss meeting his gaze. He had no doubts that he was hearing true words. 'Why are you tellin' me this?' he asked, puzzled.

'A man, if he has pride,' Jackson said, stone-faced, 'has a line he won't step over. I've reached that line, Mr Hethridge. As a cowman I rate sodbusters no higher than I would stinkin' sheep men and I'd willingly burn down their barns and destroy their crops to clear them off what oughta be good longhorn grassland. That don't mean I condone killing them and putting their womenfolk and kids in danger. Not even to satisfy Ketchum's twisted pride. That's the line I'm talkin' about, the one I don't intend crossin'.' Jackson gave a lopsided grin. 'You'll need all the edge you can get, a man and a boy going up against four killing men, so I'd advise you to swing well clear of those hills ahead of you, those wild boys will be holed-up there till they're ready to make their moves.'

Jackson drew his horse's head round and lashing at the maverick with his looped lariat, he said, 'Move, critter, move, before the irons get cold,' leaving Sam no chance to thank him for his information.

★ ★ ★

Sam took Jackson's advice and rode well clear of the range of hills. Though much against his natural urge to get to the widow Fischer's farm as fast as he could, he and Chester rode at a steady trot, as men with nothing more pressing on their minds but to get from one place to another for business that wasn't urgent. Two riders haring mad-assed across the territory, Sam knew, would raise dust and get the natural-born suspicious-minded killers, the Craddock boys, coming down from their hole-up to check them out. Then the woman he had developed strong feelings for would lose her house, and the way the Craddocks operated, probably her life as well.

Sam had told Chester about the information the Double Star straw boss had told him, but had kept his feelings towards the widow Fischer to himself. Chester had never seen his partner look so savage-faced. He was almost too scared to speak to him. The widow woman, he opined, had sure made an impression on the hard-nosed Mr Hethridge. Then, thinking things through, so had Miss Emmylou Douglas on him, and if she had been in danger then, by hell, he would be feeling just like his partner looked.

The first person Chester saw when they rode up to the widow's shack was Miss Emmylou. He wanted to feel joyful at seeing her again but knowing what kind of trouble could soon be coming along their back trail soon soured his good spirits. And Emmylou's welcoming smile faded just as quickly seeing Chester and Mr

Hethridge's grim faces.

Kate Fischer came out on to the porch as they were dismounting and her happiness at seeing Sam was also as short-lived. 'Trouble, Mr Hethridge?' she asked.

'Bad trouble, Mrs Fischer,' Sam replied. 'Both of you have to leave here, pronto. I — ' Sam broke off speaking and cocked his head. 'Are those kids' voices I'm hearin'?'

'Yes,' said Kate. 'It's the Caxton boys. Their mother is with them, she's getting them ready for bed. They've been staying with me since the day their pa was killed. Emmylou regularly rides here to help us out.'

Sam cursed under his breath. There was a whole wagonload of vulnerable people to be evacuated. 'Tell Mrs Caxton to get their clothes back on and gather up her things ready to move out as soon as we can get a horse hitched to that wagon. See to that, Marshal,' he snapped. The womenfolk and the children's lives he held in his hands was unnerving him.

'I'll help you, Chester,' Emmylou said, giving Chester a brief, apprehensive smile to hide her fearful thoughts that Chester and Mr Hethridge were going to stay and risk their lives fighting off the raiders.

'I'll go inside to give Mrs Caxton a hand to get the boys dressed.' Kate said. She stared hard at Sam. 'By your look, Mr Hethridge, you and that new pard of yours intend staying here and making a fight of it. I'm staying with you. You know my strong feelings on this matter so it is no good you wasting time, time you haven't got to squander, to persuade me otherwise. If the raiders are coming, they'll come in the dark and that's only a couple of hours away.'

She turned and walked inside, leaving Sam to ponder over just how stubborn-minded some females were. Yet grudgingly proud that the woman he longed getting closer to had the true grit of a plainswoman.

The wagon and its passengers were ready to move out. Emmylou, worried about Chester and Mr Hethridge taking on four brutal killers, asked if they wanted her pa and Jem to come and back them up in defending the house.

'It will be dark before they could make it here, Miss Emmylou,' Sam said. 'And if the shootin's started they wouldn't know who to cut loose at. You're doin' your bit by gettin' this family to safety.'

Impulsively, Emmylou kissed a surprised Chester full on the lips then, stifling a sob, she climbed up on to the wagon seat and picked up the reins. Both Sam and Chester felt a wave of relief roll over them as the wagon, rattling and bouncing, started on his way.

'Now it's up to us, pard,' Sam said. He looked Chester in the eyes. 'Scared?' he asked.

'Mr Hethridge,' replied a strain-faced

Chester, 'I would be lying if I said I wasn't scared stiff, it not being a fair fight coming our way.'

Sam laughed. 'We ain't about to do any fightin', boy. What we're goin' to do is to gun down some sonsuvbitches who have been due for plantin' years ago. They'll be dead before they know what hell they've rode into. It'll be all over in a matter of seconds, you'll see.' It better be, Sam thought. Surprise was the only edge they had. If they lost that and it turned into an outgunned shoot-out, both of them and Kate Fischer could end up dead. 'Get the horses in the barn out of sight, pard,' he said. 'And check your guns' loads.' He grinned. 'I'll go inside and try and tell that good lady she oughta do what I'm goin' to tell her.'

Kate had two mugs of steaming hot coffee ready when Sam walked in, his face still showing his strong disapproval about her decision to stay. Sam eased his conscience by telling himself he hadn't the right to make the widow do anything she didn't want to do. It was her home and that was it. The widow made matters worse for him by saying that she would show herself on the porch until it became dark so as to fool any possible watchers that everything was normal.

Not meeting her gaze, Sam growled 'Me and the boy expect to do the killin' outside, Mrs Fischer, so keep low. Shells will be flyin' which way and every way. If we fail to down them all you don't stay here, understand?' Sam lifted his head and Indian-eyed her. 'Don't have the crazy thought you can hold them off! Those sonsuvbitches don't show mercy to anyone.' Sam stormed out of the shack, softly cursing as the hot coffee splashed out of the mugs over his hands.

In spite of her fears that her stubborness to stay on her land could get Sam killed, Kate smiled. Why, she thought, I think the hard-nosed *hombre* is kind of fond of me. Then, sober-faced once more, she hoped that Sam's kid partner, whoever he was, knew the killing business well. It was too late in the day for Sam to teach him.

The Craddock gang made their move two hours after nightfall, one man, on foot. Sam, crouching in the deeper darkness of the barn entrance, heard rather than saw the raider as he scouted out the land in front of the shack. Phil Craddock was taking no chances, Sam thought. Though if luck stayed with him the raiders were going to get it mightily, and bloodily, wrong this time. Sam prayed that the kid would hold his nerve and not forget the orders he had given, not to fire until he opened the ball. If he panicked now, then it could be the Craddock gang wiping them out.

Chester also heard the prowler and the sweat poured out of him. What should he do if the raider spotted him? Cold-cock him with his pistol? With his hand sticky with sweat, he damn well wouldn't be able to hold his pistol. This law-enforcing business was getting tougher on his nerves by the day. Then, thankfully, the rustling in the brush began to fade. Chester dried the palms of his hands on his pants and pulled out his pistol and thumbed back the hammer. He put on a bold face. The killing time Mr Hethridge spoke of was about to start and it was time he stood tall.

This time there was no sneaking in. Sam could clearly hear the sound of horses. He fisted his two pistols and prepared himself for some fast and accurate shooting. He thin-smiled. He reckoned his partner would be relieved, somewhat, now the shooting was about to begin.

Bert thumbed a match into flame and touched off the oil-soaked torch. Its fiery light gave Sam four clearly seen targets. He sprang up and pulled off pistol loads with almost the non-stop rapidity of a Gatling gun. Out of the corner of one eye he saw the flashes of his partner's pistol.

The hail of lead cut into the gang, Bert being the first raider to die. Dead, with his chest ripped apart, before his brain registered he had been hit, the torch dropping from his hand as he slid sideways out of his saddle. The lighted torch brushed the flank of Josh's horse as it fell to the ground causing it to rear, snorting with pain.

Josh, clinging tight to the reins with both hands to keep his seat, couldn't get at his pistol. He managed to get out a split-second of dirty-mouthing before dying as fast as Bert had as shells tore into his neck and head. His mount's kicking and stamping feet snuffed out the torch bringing almost absolute darkness once more, and saving his brother's life. Phil saw his chance to escape death. He jabbed his spurs into his horse's ribs and, hanging along its right flank, Indian style, sped away from the killing ground, his only priority to save his own life.

Charlie, with a barrage of shells whizzing by him too close for his peace of mind, decided it was quitting time and, like Phil, tried to take advantage of the darkness to effect his escape. Chester caught a fleeting glimpse of his bulky silhouette in the saddle and fired his last pistol load at him. It was a lucky shot but not so for Charlie. The shell hit him between the shoulder-blades throwing him across his saddle horn. Charlie held on to his seat for a few more yards before choking on his own blood from his torn lungs, then rolled off his mount to land on the ground with a bone-cracking thud, a painful impact which he was past feeling.

Kate crouched under the window, shotgun gripped tight in white-knuckled fingers, every shot making her flinch as though the shells were ripping through her flesh. Suddenly the firing ceased, the silence as nerve-racking to her as the sound of the guns. Regardless of what Sam had told her, she stood up. She had to find out how Sam and his young pard had fared in the fight and taking the fearful chance of confronting one of the raiders on her porch, she stepped outside, ready to pull off both barrels if it was needed.

'Get back inside, Mrs Fischer!' she heard Sam yell.

'There's one of the bastards still up on his horse! Me and the boy are gonna flush him out!'

A happy, sobbing Kate did as she was told and, as she closed the door behind her, she wondered why she had done so. It wasn't as though Mr Hethridge was her husband. Though that wouldn't be a crazy idea, Kate thought, if a bad-ass loner could be persuaded to settle down and work a dirt farm. Kate snorted. And she would invite Ketchum to the wedding.

'He's gone, Mr Hethridge,' Chester said. 'I missed him, but got the other sonuvabitch who tried cut and run with him.'

'Good work,' said Sam. 'Are you OK!'

'Yeah, not a scratch on me,' replied Chester.

Sam grinned. 'I told you it would be a piece of cake, boy. But we'd better check on the fellas we shot just to make sure they'll not bother Christian folk again. Then you ride to the Douglas place and put their minds at ease. I reckon they must be worryin' about us.'

What nervous reactions Chester was having after the shooting vanished at the pleasant, cocky thought of how the sweet-smiling Emmylou would look on him when she heard the good news. Though Chester was honest enough to himself to have nagging doubts whether or not his nerves would stand up to regular shoot-outs with outlaw gangs without the expertise of Mr Hethridge or Marshal Bellwood to stiffen up his backbone.

Sam was also having pleasant thoughts of his own when he told the widow Fischer she was no longer in danger. He smiled. That's if she forgave him for bawling at her.

Once clear of the farm, Phil had swung back into his saddle. He hadn't fired back at the ambushers, that would come later at his own choosing. Then, by hell, he would make the sodbusters pay in blood for the killing of Josh and the wiping out of his gang. Cursing the sodbusters would have to do until it was getting-even day. Phil's horse stumbled, then its speed dropped to a limping walk. A mad-eyed Phil's cursing became more profane as he felt the warm stickiness of blood on his mount's right shoulder. He would have to get himself a fresh horse or his day of reckoning with the sodbusters wouldn't dawn. Belle Star had a spare horse, he recollected. He gave a grimace of a smile. And going free as well.

★   ★   ★

It was dawn, a cold damp daybreak, by the time Phil made it to Younger's Bend on a horse that could scarcely lift its wounded leg. When happy, Phil wasn't the most sociable of men but now, losing his brother and his two men and the ignominy of riding blindly into a trap like some greenhorn city dude, his cold hatred bordered on the edge of insanity. If anyone, man, woman or child upset him any further he would gut shoot them.

All was quiet at the house when Phil dismounted at the corral. Expecting to do some hard, fast riding, the big rangy bay would have to be his choice. He drew out his pistol and walked across to the shack where Belle Starr's fetch-and-carry hand slept. And was still that way as he heard the sound of snoring coming through the open door. He stepped quietly inside and brought his pistol down hard on the sleeping man's head. The snoring stopped immediately and the man sank deeper into his cot. Phil gave a grunt of satisfaction. He would be halfway across the territory before the old goat came to, if he ever did wake up. There was only Belle Starr to be dealt with if she showed up and got awkward.

Belle came out on to the porch as Phil was fastening his saddle on his new horse. She was still wearing her night clothes. She stood there, arms behind her back, hard-eying Phil.

'I always took you and your so-called 'gang' to be two-bit horse-thieves, Phil,' she said. 'Unless, of course you were coming up to the house to pay me for the horse before you rode out. And by none of your boys being with you I reckon you've made a balls-up of what Ketchum paid you to do.' Belle shook her head. 'That's the worst of hiring a bunch of back-shooting road agents to do real shootingmen's work.'

'You no-good bitch!' yelled Phil. Flecks of spit bubbling at the corners of his mouth. He grabbed for his pistol.

Belle brought her right hand from behind her back and the long-barrelled pistol it held barked and flamed, bucking in her hand as it discharged. The heavy ball punched a red-rimmed hole in the centre of Phil's forehead, its impact spinning him away from the horse and on the road to hell to meet up with the rest of the Craddock gang.

I always opined, Belle thought, as she

lowered her gun, that the new breed of outlaws aren't worth a spit. Mr Hethridge would be risking a hanging having those assholes as partners.

13

The brightness of the early morning sun shining through the window woke up Sam with a start. Bleary-eyed, he glanced at the empty chair alongside him, the one in which Kate Fischer had sat keeping watch with him. He felt guilty at falling asleep when he was supposed to be guarding her home, and annoyed, slightly, at the widow draping a blanket over his shoulders as though he was an over-the-hill old fart, which, on reflection, he was well on the way to becoming. He was tired and the way he had been lying asleep in the chair his wound had begun to ache again, and bleed once more. He was definitely getting too old to exchange lead with a bunch of bad-ass raiders.

He had gone into the shack to tell the widow she was safe and could get herself to bed, though he would stay in the cabin keeping watch on the off-chance that the raider who had escaped death might be a man who bore strong grudges and try to sneak back to seek revenge for the killing of his partners.

'It's only right and proper I should stand guard alongside you, Mr Hethridge,' the widow Fischer had said. 'It is my home.' Kate smiled. 'And, besides, after all that's gone on around here I don't think I could sleep. And I can keep the coffee hot.'

Sam didn't argue. He already knew the widow had a mind of her own. And he would have thought he had misjudged her character if she hadn't offered to stand guard with him. He had sat alongside females at gambling tables, stood with them at bars while they downed drink for drink, and lay with them, jaybird naked, but none of them had given him the same pleasure as sitting alongside the middle-aged widow woman Kate Fischer.

They didn't talk much. What small

talk could a former bank robber, ex-con, talk about to a gentle female, Sam thought? And Kate wondered if she dared tell the man she had strong feelings for that she had worked in a Kansas sporting house. So there they sat, watchful yet settled in mutual satisfaction.

Sam was sitting back digesting his breakfast, thinking how easy he could fit in the way of having his meals cooked for him and laid out on a table, if a woman was crazy enough to do it for him, when he heard Kate say from the kitchen, that she could see the dust of a wagon coming in. Sam's brief, pleasant interlude from the war against Ketchum was over. The rancher, although he had suffered a couple of heavy setbacks wouldn't quit until he had been forced on to his knees and lost all the will to fight for what he wanted, and he had to be ready to meet those new threats.

Both of them were on the porch to greet Jim Douglas and two more farmers, the three heavily armed, and Marshal Chester Willis with Emmylou Douglas sitting up behind him on his horse.

Kate smiled. 'Your young pard has certainly taken a shine to Miss Emmylou.'

'I don't think that shine will last very long,' Sam replied dourly. 'Not if the kid sticks to his foolhardy notion of wantin' to be one of Judge Parker's marshals. What killin' he's seen so far oughta put him off wearin' a badge.'

Kate tried not to think too much on the fact that Mr Hethridge, in the present situation, could not have high hopes of a future, pleasant or otherwise.

'And you don't think we farmers are free of any more trouble from Ketchum, Sam?' Jim Douglas said, on hearing Sam telling them that they must still remain on their guard. The three sober-faced farmers exchanged apprehensive looks. All the men were crowded in Kate's living-room reviewing the situation along the creek. The farmers, hoping against hope that they had bloodied Ketchum's nose enough for him to be satisfied with the land he already owned. Kate and Emmylou were feeding the hogs and the hens, keeping well away from the barn where Sam had dragged the bodies of the dead raiders until graves had been dug for them.

'No, I don't,' replied Sam. 'I don't expect any more raids like we had last night bein' that some of his crew don't see eye to eye with their boss's tactics of using hired killers to get what he wants. But Ketchum's ambitious and his twisted pride is at stake. And, as the sonuvabitch has already proved, some men will do anything to hang on to their pride, even get themselves killed for it.'

'We'll take your advice, Sam,' Jim Douglas said. 'I'll pass the word along the crick that it isn't standing-down time yet.'

'You do that, Jim,' Sam said. He smiled. 'And I'll get on with my private beef against Ketchum.' He looked across the table at Chester. 'And this time it really means me. You're wearin' a peace-officer's badge and you'll lose that, and your liberty, if not your life, goin' up against Ketchum openly with a double murderer. Stay here and back up the farmers; do what you're paid to do, keep the peace.'

Though he was disappointed at not being allowed to ride with his partner, Chester knew Mr Hethridge was talking sense. Two men travelling across dangerous territory doubled the possibility of them being seen, and shot dead by the Ketchum's men.

'OK, Mr Hethridge. 'But take care.' He grinned. 'Being I'm not there to watch your ass.'

'You ain't tryin' to throw a scare into an old man, boy?' a smiling Sam replied. 'Now I'll go and get my horse saddled up and move out.'

There was another problem he hadn't told the farmers about that wanted clearing up, the whereabouts of the last raider. Until he was dead he could be a threat. There was a chance he could have gone back to Younger's Bend so it would be worthwhile making another call on Belle Starr.

On hearing the news that Sam was going to wage a one-man war against the Double Star, Kate had the sinking feeling she was destined to be a widow for the rest of her life. Mr Hethridge's pride was as stupid as Ketchum's and would get him killed. And she couldn't see another kind, elderly German on the horizon offering to marry her.

'We'll see to those bastards lying there in the barn, Sam,' Jim Douglas said. 'We'll take them into Spine Ridge, put 'em on display. When Ketchum hears of it he could consider he's bitten off more than he can swallow. That it isn't going to be easy for him to shift us sodbusters off our farms.'

'It sure won't make him any happier,' replied Sam. 'But as I said, Ketchum is a takin' man and he'll come up with another plan for him to get your land.

I'll try and warn you if I get a smell of what his next moves are.'

It gave Sam much comfort noticing that Kate Fischer didn't look too happy at him riding out all on his own to fight the sodbusters' battle. If he had told her that he was going to try his damnedest to burn down the rancher's fine house he had the feeling she would have yanked him out of his saddle to stop him from going. He never thought he would be an answer to a lonely fine-looking widow's dreams. Sam's lips twitched in the ghost of a smile. And then again he could be just plumb loco thinking such way-out thoughts.

'Don't forget, you sodbusters,' he said. 'Don't drop your guard.' Then he cast a beaming, confident smile at the 'lonely widow'. He kneed his horse into moving and rode out, leaving all on the porch wondering if they would ever see him again.

★ ★ ★

On his approach to Younger's Bend, Sam noticed an elderly man busy digging on a bare ridge alongside the Canadian. Mrs Belle Starr was in the corral grooming one of the two horses it held. Belle turned as he pulled up at the fence.

'Why, if it isn't Mr Hethridge,' Belle said. 'I'd figured you be well on the way to Texas by now.'

Sam gave her a twisted-faced grin. 'Well, I kinda thought I'd have one last try to get hold of Phil Craddock. Or any of his boys for that matter, to put that proposition of mine to them. Have any of them swung by this way, ma'am?'

'It's funny you should ask that,' replied Belle. 'Phil himself called on me earlier in the day.' Belle smiled. 'You could say that he's kinda still here.'

A puzzled Sam jerked up in his saddle. 'Kind of, ma'am?' His hand dropped down to his pistol butt, a movement not unnoticed by Belie.

'Yeah,' said Belle. 'He's up there.' She

pointed at the ridge. 'My hired hand is burying the no-good horse-thief. The sonuvabitch tried to help himself to this bay I'm grooming, so I shot him. Phil seemed mightily put out when he came in and his brother and the two fellas who tagged along as his pards weren't with him.' Belle gave Sam a long, eyebrow-raised look. 'You wouldn't have anything to do with that, would you, Mr Hethridge?'

Sam grinned. 'Now, why would you think that of me, ma'am?' replied Sam. 'When I was hopin' those boys could have helped me out.'

Belle laughed. 'And I'm the most sought-after female in the Nations.' She favoured Sam with another one of her long, searching, quizzical looks. 'You wouldn't be a stinking Pinkerton, or a bounty-hunter, Mr Hethridge?'

'I ain't sunk that low to be a lawman of any sort, Mrs Starr,' Sam said. 'I am who I said I was, a one-time bank robber. And I don't look kindly on horse-thieves so I ain't sheddin' any tears on Phil's sudden demise. You were entitled to plug the sonuvabitch. And I will tell you this: you needn't worry about his brother, or the other two fellas, ridin' in here seekin' retribution for killin' Phil. They've gone to the same place Phil has.' He touched the brim of his hat in a farewell gesture and tugged at the reins. 'It's nice to have made your acquaintance, ma'am,' he said, as his mount pulled way from the corral. Straight-faced he added, 'It seems I'll have to look elsewhere to raise me a gang.'

A thoughtful Belle Starr watched him ride out. Whatever else you are, Mr Hethridge, you're one helluva liar. You're not after raising a gang, but what business you have in the Nations seems to be going your way, so far.

14

Jackson didn't go up to the big house when the news was brought in that three of his boss's latest hirings were laid out on planks in the undertaker's parlour at Spine Ridge. He left that unpalatable chore to the ranch-hand who had seen the dead raiders, not wanting risking getting shot by Ketchum if he told him the bad news.

He was surprised how calm Ketchum seemed when he came out on to the porch and called him over. Only when he came face to face with his boss did Jackson realize somehow Ketchum was bottling in his anger. The mad, crazy rage he was feeling only showed in his wide, glaring eyes.

'Get all the ranch-hands here mounted up, pronto, Jackson,' Ketchum barked. 'Then round up the two nearest herds. If you want a goddamned job doing,

Jackson, don't rely on the hired hands. See to it yourself.' The smile he gave his straw boss matched the crazy look in his eyes. 'I aim to pay a call on those stinking sodbusters, Texas style. We'll stampede those longhorns right along the creek, stamping as many of their shacks and growing crops into the dirt. By thunder we'll leave a dust bowl behind us.'

Jackson had to do some controlling of his own, to keep the shock and disbelief from showing in his face for what his boss was contemplating. Several hundred head of high-tailing longhorns would not only grind into kindling any building in their way but crush to death every man, woman or child unfortunate enough to be in their path. The mad-ass glare he was getting from Ketchum warned him that if he hesitated carrying out his orders he would wind up dead here on the big-house porch.

'Right away, boss,' he said, and began shouting out his orders, thinking that whatever trouble the bank robber Hethridge had gone to in practically wiping out the Craddock gang had been a waste of shells. No one could stop a herd of spooked longhorns from flattening everything before them. Jackson shrugged. He had helped the sodbusters all he could; it was now up to God, if He was so inclined, to come up with a miracle to save them.

Sam saw the converging clouds of dust ahead of him and began to wonder why. He was no cowman but he knew that it wasn't the trailing season to the railhead town. Then he thought that maybe Ketchum was moving his cows on to fresh grass. Though that likelihood didn't rest easy with him. Grim-faced, he nosed his mount into a deep dry wash that snaked its way in the general direction of the dust clouds. He could be spotted by one of the Double Star crew but it was a risk that had to be taken to confirm his fearful thoughts of what tactic Ketchum was going to use next to clear the sodbusters off their farms. If he was right, then by heck, he would have to do some hard riding to warn the farmers that hell in the shape of thousands of pounding hooves was coming in close behind him.

The wash got him within tasting distance of the dust clouds and Sam thought it was wiser to go the rest of the way on foot. He drew out his rifle, dismounted and walked a few paces along the wash until he found a place where he could climb the sandy bank without slipping back down. He had heard that wisdom comes to a man as he aged. Not in his case; he was becoming more foolish. He was really having a one-man war with the Double Star. And, if he was spotted, his crazy war would only last as long as he could run before a ranch-hand put a bullet in his back.

He peered over the rim of the wash close enough to hear the shouts of the men herding the cows in the direction they wanted them to go and close enough to the back of a single rider he recognized as the Double Star straw boss bellowing to his men working on the flanks of the herd. Sam took another chance; that of hoping the straw boss hadn't run out of giving favours to the sodbusters.

He waited for the flank men to ride further away from his wash before he called out, 'It's me, Hethridge! I've got a rifle aimed at your back just in case you ain't as friendly as you were the first time we met. If you are, are those longhorns bein' gathered up for what I think they are?' Sam waited, first pressure of the trigger taken up, as he watched for the straw boss's reaction to his call.

Jackson dismounted and walked towards the edge of the wash stopping several yards to Sam's left then opened his flies and relieved himself. Not looking at Sam, he said, 'You'd better ass-kick it back to the crick, Hethridge, and get those sodbusters and their kin up on to high ground. Ketchum, as you've figured, is cutting loose his cows, a whole bunch of them. I'll try and hold them back as long as I can, but Ketchum is calling the shots here. He's on the far side of the herd, and he's gone loco.'

Jackson buttoned up his pants and started back to his horse, Sam slithered down to the bottom of the wash, cursing. He was supposed to have been helping the farmers and all he had done was to see them about to lose everything they possessed, even their lives if he couldn't warn them in time.

Sam rib-kicked his mount along the wash, risking being unsaddled and breaking his neck galloping over the loose stones. He still wasn't making as fast a time as he would have done riding across open country, but he'd had a difficult choice to make. It wouldn't help the sodbusters any if, by riding across open territory, his trail dust was seen by any of the Double Star crew. The hunt for him would be in earnest. He would never make it to the creek. He only hoped the straw boss would win him the time he promised.

The wash took a sharp turn to Sam's right and began to shallow, allowing him to see over its edge. In the same direction, across some 200 yards of sun-yellowed grass, he saw a long rocky ridge. Sam yanked at his reins, and as his mount drew up in a flurry of stones and dust he took an assaying look at the territory.

Sam was eyeing a bottleneck, an ideal spot where a bunch of men firing pistols could turn the herd and send it scattering back to the Double Star range. Or something just as off-putting to the cows, one man could do. Sam's face lost some of its tension. Something like a fire, he thought. He was still some distance from the nearest farm, so he opined Ketchum wouldn't stampede the herd until they were well clear of the bottleneck. So he had time to do what was necessary. He would spook the herd for Ketchum, but not in the direction he intended.

He got down from his horse and scrambled up the side of the wash and walked several yards across the flat, testing which way the wind was blowing. Sam didn't want the fire he was about to start to burn at his ass. Satisfied that the strong breeze was gusting in his favour and he had not yet seen the ominous dust clouds heading his way, he squatted down and began removing Colt loads from his gunbelt.

Using his knife, he prised the cases from the shells and tipped the black powder on the ground between his knees. After several minutes, cursing occasionally as the knife slipped and drew blood on his fingers, Sam suddenly felt the ground tremble slightly beneath him. He glanced up and saw the dust of Ketchum's live battering ram coming in, he judged, at a steady lope. What powder he had would have to do. The grass was dry enough to burn like the fires of Hell once the flames took hold; the gunpowder would see to that.

Sam dropped back down into the wash to wait until he could clearly hear the drumming hoofs of the cows. It was past the worrying stage, he had run out of time. If his crackpot plan failed, the sodbusters were doomed. Muttering a distant memory of a prayer, he touched off the thin powder trail with a lighted match and watched its spluttering fiery track with the fixed hypnotic gaze of a jackrabbit being eyeballed by a rattler.

At first, Sam could only see wisps of smoke from the burnt-out powder behind the creeping flame and did some more cursing, thinking that he had never done as much cursing when he was being chased by gun-shooting sheriffs' posses. His hope now lay in the small handful of powder at the end of the trail. Surely, he wildly hoped, the flaring flames that it would make should set the grass alight. And it couldn't come too soon; it would only be a matter of minutes before the longhorns pounded through the bottleneck. Suddenly candlewick-size flames licked up the tufts of grass and, as the wind caught them, they blossomed red and angry, and spread. The pile of powder exploded in a dull popping noise, like the sound of a small-calibre pistol discharge. The yellow-tinged flames shot two feet into the air, doing what Sam had prayed for. The ragged line of flame and smoke raced across the bottleneck to the foot of the rocky high ground, then began to widen, spreading towards the incoming herd.

The first of the cattle, with the pressure of the rest of the herd behind them, snorting and bellowing in fear, leapt through the fiery barrier. The rest managed to turn and, in a compact wedge of heaving, high-kicking bodies, thundered back the way they had been driven, trampling riders and their horses not fast enough to get out their way, into a mash of blood and bone. Some of the terrified cows spilled over into the wash. Sam had to leap into his saddle and ride his horse out on to the flat to escape injury.

There he sat behind the high wall of drifting smoke that masked the flames, smiling as he contemplated his handiwork. His prayers, he thought, had been answered, in spades. He only hoped he hadn't started a blaze that would burn off half the grass in the Nations. Sam decided to push his good luck to the limit. Banking that every hand, even the cook's cat, on the Double Star payroll would be out to stop the stampeding longhorns from fire-balling out of the territory, he ought to have no problem in sneaking on to the Double Star range and putting a match to Ketchum's fine house.

The damage he would have inflicted on Ketchum, his cows scattered to hell and beyond, his house a burnt-out ruin, would take Ketchum months, maybe years, to build up again and take his mind off his need to grab the sodbusters' land for ever. Ketchum's anger and rage at his humiliation would be directed at him, but he would make it his business to be a long ways from the territory, too far for Ketchum to do anything but curse him.

A stone-faced, exhausted Jackson slumped forward in his saddle. He wished he had been a sheep man and never seen a stinking longhorn. The ornery critters would see him in an early grave. He was lucky that time hadn't come right now. Four of his men and six good cow ponies hadn't been so lucky, They lay broken-boned, hammered into the ground in the wake of the stampeding herd. Mr Hethridge was one real hell-raiser.

The son-of-a-bitch had caused Ketchum more grief in a couple of weeks than the Comanche had done in all the years he had worked on the ranch. Jackson hoped that the crazy, arrogant bastard, Ketchum, would realize he had lost his war against the sodbusters, or he would have no crew left to boss over.

'Get those damn cows rounded up, Jackson,' Ketchum had shouted, sitting up in his fine saddle with his horse shedding blood on both of its flanks, 'before they're to hell and gone!'

He had almost had the guts to tell Ketchum he'd had his bellyful of fighting his war, but Ketchum had pulled his horse away and ridden back to the Double Star to tend to his blood-line horse's wounds. How long did Ketchum think it would take to round up the scattered longhorns with the few men he had, Jackson thought, bushed as they were, and down in the dumps at losing their bunkhouse pals. The cows would have to be weeded out of every canyon and draw between here and the Kansas border.

'Pike, you and Lester,' he said, 'bury what's left of the boys here, put a marker on their graves. Collect what gear's of any use and take it back to the ranch. Then bring out some rations, water, and the rest of the boys, and catch us up.' Jackson gave a mirthless grin. 'We sure gonna earn our due the hard way over the next few days.'

15

Sam gave the house and the outbuildings a careful-eyed scrutiny. The place seemed deserted. It was as he had surmised, all the hands were out rounding up their boss's cows. He reckoned that in the time that would take he could dismantle Ketchum's big house plank by plank and cart it away without being disturbed. He dismounted, but, not prepared to take any unnecessary chances, his pistol was fisted and he approached the house under cover of the barns.

Sam had kept to the wash as long as he could on the ride to the Double Star. What he could see of his fire coming up on to the flat was only a dark line of smoke. The land between the wash and the end of the high ground had widened and it gave him some satisfaction to see that it was bare, stony ground, a fire break, if the flames got this far. He had not set the Nations on fire.

As Sam passed one building he heard the rattle of pans and a man chanting in a sing-song voice. He paused for several seconds, gun and nerves ready, to shoot his way out of trouble. The ranch wasn't deserted after all. On hearing no more voices, Sam opined that the cook must be on his own, so pressed on to the back of the ranch house. By the time the cook saw the flames the inside of the house should be well ablaze and could do nothing about it except watch it burn.

Sam stepped through the unlocked back door and took a quick look around. The fine furnishings and carpets made him think that it was a shame to burn down such a grand house that folk had raised a sweat, not Ketchum's, to build. Now Ketchum was spilling sodbusters' blood to maintain his high style of living. The sodbusters were entitled to take some of that style from him any way they could.

Sam walked over carpets thick enough to deaden his footsteps into what he reckoned, by the big desk and padded armchair behind it, to be Ketchum's den. He grinned wolfishly. He couldn't have picked a better spot to start the fire. The heavy drapes at the window would act as a powder fuse.

Ketchum had finished tending to his blood horse's wounds and was walking across to the corral to saddle up one of the remuda prior to riding out to check what progress Jackson and the crew were making gathering in the long-horns. A casual glance at the ranch house froze him dead in his tracks. He was seeing a flickering red glow behind the windows of his den, a sight he could hardly believe. The son-of-a-bitch Hethridge had the gall to burn his house down. Snarling obscenities, he drew out his pistol. The saddle-tramp had walked into his house; he would see to it he was dragged out by the heels,

Boot Hill carrion.

Sam, watching pieces of the burning drapes dropping on to the thick pile carpet, starting new fires, didn't know of his danger until he felt a cold breeze at the back of his neck. Spinning round, owlhoot-warning nerves twanging, he saw Ketchum standing straddle-legged in the doorway aiming his pistol at him smiling a savage grimace of victory. He flung himself sideways as the rancher fired, gasping with pain as he felt a mule-like kick in his right side. Though half-blinded with tears of pain, Sam was still capable of fighting back. He snapped off two rapid shots at Ketchum before the cursing rancher, his target obscured by the now billowing smoke, could fire off the killing shot. Two shots that put Ketchum past worrying about his fine house burning to the ground and his ambition to own the sod-busters' land forever.

Sam, leaning against the desk for support, saw that the doorway was clear. He didn't know if he had downed the rancher or he had just dodged out of his line of fire. Whatever, he had to get out of the den, out of the house, or he would go up in flames with it. A bullet from Ketchum would be a less painful death. He staggered, agonizingly slowly, to the door, the heat from the flames singeing the back of his coat and pants. Just outside the doorway he saw Ketchum's crumpled body. The relief at knowing he had shot true gave Sam the extra strength to make it out of the house seconds before a sheet of flame roared out of the den and set fire to the hall ceiling.

On hearing the shooting, the Chinese cook came to the cookhouse door holding a big cleaver. The man who stumbled out of his boss's house didn't look like a man. With his face smoke-blackened and twisted, clothes smouldering and flames pouring out of the windows behind him he looked like a devil coming up out of a white man's hell. And it didn't need the pistol the 'devil' waved at him to convince him he had urgent chores to do back inside.

Somehow, Sam got astride his mount feeling as old as Methuselah and ready for his grave. He took one last look at what was now Ketchum's funeral pyre before heading back to the creek and the healing hands of Widow Fischer, if he didn't pass out and fall out of his saddle on the way there.

16

It was a fretful Kate Fischer who kept coming out on to the porch gazing anxiously across the creek for signs of Mr Hethridge riding in. It would be dark in a couple of hours and he would have to spend another night God knows where risking his life for her and the other farmers.

She could see that young Chester was as worried about the well-being of his partner as she was. He had hardly paid heed to Emmylou Douglas who had called on them an hour or so ago with the disturbing news from a farmer whose land was west of her pa's place, that he'd seen grass fires five, six miles distance from his farm.

Kate's heart had sunk. The fires meant that Mr Hethridge had failed in his mad-ass attempt to stop Ketchum's hired guns putting the torch to some poor sodbuster's home. A failure, knowing the ex-bank-robber's character, that meant he was dead or captured by Ketchum.

'It can't be a farm, Mrs Fischer,' Emmylou said. 'It's open range where the fires are. That's what's puzzling Pa.'

Kate grinned widely. The old hellion was still alive! The fires could only be Mr Hethridge's doing and for some real purpose. Then her spirits dropped again. Mr Hethridge's fire raising must have happened hours ago. Anything could have happened since then. Ketchum would be moving heaven and earth to hunt him down.

Chester cursing, silently, his stubborn old fart of a partner for leaving him here to guard Mrs Fischer's property when he should have been by his side, had had a bellyful of chewing at his nails with worry. Even the presence of Emmylou wasn't calming him down.

'I'll ride along the trail apiece, Mrs Fischer,' he said. 'Get up on some high ground to see if I can see any signs of

Mr Hethridge, or warn you if any Double Star men are heading this way.'

'And I'll come with you, Chester,' Emmylou said, fearing that the boy she intended to marry was crazy enough to ride off on to Ketchum's range to seek out his partner. Her lips hardened into twin hard lines. By golly, she thought, she would try every female wile she knew, or heard from other girls, to prevent him from doing that.

The pair of them had barely cleared the creek when Chester saw the familiar white-nosed horse coming towards them, its rider almost bent double in his saddle.

'Go back to Mrs Fischer, Emmylou,' he said. 'Tell her Mr Hethridge is riding in! And she has to get water boiling; it looks as though he's been wounded.' He kicked his horse savagely in the ribs to ride at a mad gallop to his partner, fearing the worst.

Sam opened pain-glazed eyes as Chester came alongside him, Chester wincing as he noticed the dark patch on

Sam's right side.

'Are you hit badly, Mr Hethridge?' he asked worriedly, reaching out a hand to steady his partner in the saddle.

'I ain't as sorely wounded as I was that day in Kansas when those lawmen cut us all down,' replied Sam. 'Though to speak truly I hurt like hell. I must be gettin' old. And then again I ain't as badly off as Ketchum. He's well and truly dead.' Sam gave a ghost of a smile. 'Straighten me up in the saddle, boy. I don't favour that widow woman giving me one of her I-told-you-so looks when I call on her.'

★   ★   ★

It had been two days since Sam had returned to Kate's house and now, shirtless, sitting in the sun with a clean bandage strapped across his middle and arm, no longer felt that a plot on Boot Hill would be a thankful blessing. Ketchum's shot had gone deep, cracking a couple of ribs before passing clear through his body. If the wound didn't get infected he would soon be back to normal. Kate, in between fussing over him as she cleaned up the wound, cursed him for being such a crazy idiot as he told her of the stampeding of the cows and the killing of Ketchum.

As the word spread along the creek that Ketchum was no longer a threat to them several farmers rode into Kate's to thank Sam for saving their livelihoods, one farmer offering to plough his growing land for him when he married the widow, until he was strong enough to manage a plough himself.

Sam grinned. Him a sodbuster? Cal Butler and the rest of the boys down there in Hell would be laughing fit to bust. He looked up and saw Kate sweet-smiling him and then thought soberly that if Cal and the gang had taken up sodbusting instead of robbing banks they would still be alive today. And he was pleased when Chester had told him he had given up his crazy notion of being one of Judge Parker's marshals. He was going back to being a sodbuster, working for Kate until he had raked up enough money to ask Mr Douglas for his daughter's hand in marriage. By hell, Sam thought, if the widow Fischer was crazy enough to marry him he would take up that sodbuster's offer to plough his land. He felt comfortable and at ease with himself for the first time in his life.

A cry from Jim Douglas of 'Two riders comin' in!' raised a ripple of tension among the farmers. Then Chester calling out 'It's OK, it's Marshal Bellwood and Sheriff Kearney!' relaxed them all again. Chester stepped down from the porch to greet them and, as he passed Sam, he gave him a boss-man's stare. 'Let me do the talking, Mr Hethridge. You just sit there, understand?'

'Understood,' replied Sam, thinking that his young pard had grown up into a man in all ways. He sat there all tensed up and the future he thought it was possible to have began to slip away.

Both lawmen swung down from their mounts. Sheriff Kearney hard-eyed Jim Douglas. 'I've heard that there's been several kinds of hell and some, raised on Ketchum's range. His cows scattered to Christ knows where and him and his grand house goin' up in smoke. You sodbusters hadn't a hand in it, did you?'

Jim Douglas gave out a caustic laugh. 'Us sodbusters taking on Ketchum's hired bully boys? We couldn't even protect our own families and properties.' He pointed over his shoulder. 'Ketchum's raiders burnt out my barns!' he said, angrily. 'And the murderous bastards killed Calvin Caxton and burnt his house down. His wife and his two boys were lucky to escape with their lives. So we sodbusters figure that Ketchum got back what he reaped and we ain't sorry. M'be now we can work our fields in peace.'

Sheriff Kearney grunted non-committally. Range wars tended to get out of hand somewhat and he was glad this one seemed to have been settled in the sodbusters' favour. He was counting on their votes when he came up for re-election. Just then, he spotted a horse with a white blaze running down its nose.

'It looks as though your young deputy got his man, Marshal,' he said. 'That horse across there, according to the late Mr Ketchum, is the one Hethridge was on when he came up to the ranch house.'

Marshal Bellwood gave Chester an amazed look. 'Is that so, boy?' he said. 'Where is he? And here's me and Judge Parker worryin' that you'd come to harm when you didn't report in after that week I gave you.'

'Yeah, well, I'm sorry about that, Mr Bellwood,' Chester said. 'But I kinda got drawn into the range war the sheriff spoke of. And as for Hethridge, well, he's buried with a couple of other owlhoots out there on the plains. Me, Mr Douglas and Mr Sloan, sitting there bandaged up, jumped them when they were trying to lift Mr Douglas's stock. That's how Mr Sloan came by his wound. Isn't that so, Mr Douglas?'

'That's the way it was, Chester,' Jim Douglas replied. 'I figure this fella Hethridge got himself a gang of sorts and taking advantage of the situation Ketchum was causing us, thought it was a good chance to get himself some easy money.'

Bellwood cast a sharp-eyed look at 'Mr Sloan' and his gun-hand began to twitch. The stone-faced Mr Sloan didn't look like a sodbuster. In fact, he had often seen suchlike visages through the back sights of his rifle. His gut feeling was that he had been lied to. Mr Sloan hadn't come by his wound that way at all.

Kate saw the marshal's doubting look and stepped close to Sam and rested a hand on his shoulder. 'Tom Sloan is my fiancé; he hails from Kansas like me. He's been staying with Mr Douglas being it's not fitting to stay here with me until we are wed. The wedding will take place in Spine Ridge as soon as Tom can get around without his wound opening up again. You and your good lady wife are invited to the ceremony, Sheriff.'

Sam couldn't believe what he had just heard. Kate Fischer was pulling him out of one hell of a tight spot. He would willingly marry her for that alone.

'I'll look forward to that day, ma'am,' Sheriff Kearney said. 'Now it's time I rode out to the Double Star to write up my report on just what the hell's been happening there. Are you staying in the territory, Marshal?'

Marshal Bellwood had already come to the conclusion that Mr Sloan, or whoever he really was, had played a big, and deadly hand, in the burning and killing spree at the Double Star ranch. He hadn't the time to prove his thinking, he had plenty of known outlaws to rope in without bothering with a man he was believing was an owlhoot. And, for a more personal reason, he was keeping his doubting thoughts about Mr Sloan to himself. The hard looks the rifle and shotgun-toting sodbusters were giving him told him it would bode ill with them if he made a move against a man who had stood by them in their fight against Ketchum's raiders.

'No,' he said. 'I'm heading back to Fort Smith. I've no papers to serve here. I only came into the territory to see how my young deputy was faring. It seems I rode here for nothing, he's done OK, a credit to the marshal service.'

'I hate to tell you this, Mr Bellwood,' Chester said. 'But I'm quitting being a marshal. I'm going back to what I really ought to be, a farmer. I only hope I'm not offending you.' He unpinned his badge and handed it to the marshal.

'No offence taken, boy,' replied Marshal Bellwood. 'I'm proud to have had you as my pard.' He grinned. 'A man would be every kind of fool there is to trade the company of that pretty young girl up there on the porch beaming away at you to share cold night camps, dodge outlaws' bullets with a sour-pussed old man. Well, it's time I was getting back to Fort Smith, or the old judge will start fretting over me.' He gave Sam a final penetrating look. 'And you don't get yourself plugged again, Mr Sloan, or that fine-looking woman you're about to get hitched to will have to do all the work herself.'

As he watched the two lawmen ride out, Sam said to Chester, 'If you hadn't lied for me, boy, that former pard of yours would have sniffed me out for sure. I know the fellas I shot were killed in a fair fight, but I would have had one helluva job to prove that. So why did you lie, bein' that we ain't been together long enough to become real pards?'

'What you have done for the farmers, risking your life and all, entitles you to some reward,' Chester said. And I reckon the good you've done for all the folk here must wipe out some of the bad things you have done in your life. You've kinda redeemed yourself more than somewhat.' Chester smiled. 'It isn't too late to get religion, Mr Hethridge.'

Sam sat back, relaxed. 'Nor get hitched, Mr Willis,' he murmured, smiling.

THE END

GUNS OF THE GAMBLER

M. Duggan

Destitute gambler Ben Crow arrives in Mallory keen to claim his inheritance, only to discover that rancher Edward Bacon has other ideas. Set up by Miss Dorothy, who had fooled him completely, Ben finds himself dangling on the end of a rope. Saved from death, Ben sets off in pursuit of Miss Dorothy, determined upon retribution. However, his quest for vengeance turns into a rescue mission when she is kidnapped by a crazy man-burning bandit.